It Falls Into Place

the stories of Phyllis Shand Allfrey

It Falls Into Place
the stories of Phyllis Shand Allfrey

Edited by Lizabeth Paravisini-Gebert

PAPILLOTE PRESS

London and Roseau, Dominica

First published in Great Britain in 2004 by Papillote Press

A CIP catalogue record for this book is available from the British Library.

Acknowledgement. The publication of this book was funded in part through a generous grant from the Vassar College Faculty Research Committee

Typeset in Book Antiqua and Century Gothic
Printed and bound in Malaysia

ISBN: 0 9532224 1 1

Papillote Press
23 Rozel Road
London SW4 OEY
United Kingdom

Also by Phyllis Shand Allfrey

The Orchid House, *first published by Constable, 1953; re-issued by Virago Press, 1982*
In Circles: poems, *London, 1940*
Palm And Oak: poems, *London, 1950*

The following stories from It Falls Into Place were first published elsewhere:

Uncle Rufus, *Tribune, December 11 1942*

A Talk On China, *The Windmill 1, no.1, 1944-46*

Breeze, *Pan Africa, January 1947*

O Stay And Hear, *Argosy 15, no 9, September 1954*

It Falls Into Place, *Dominica Herald, June 13 1964 (as Philip Warner)*

A Time For Loving, *Dominica Star, February 12 and 18, 1966*

A Real Person, *Dominica Star, June 4 and 11, 1966*

Proserpeena and the Colonel, *Dominica Star, February 4 1967*

Miss Garthside's Greenhouse, *Caribbean Women Writers: Essays from the First International Conference, edited by Selwyn Cudjoe, 1990*

Contents

Introduction

The name of Phyllis Shand Allfrey evokes contradictory images. Born in 1908 into a family of white colonial officials in the British colony of Dominica in the eastern Caribbean, she built a political career through an alliance with the labour unions and peasantry that threatened the interests of her own class and race. A promising writer whose first novel, The Orchid House (1953), opened bright prospects for a successful literary career in England, she renounced all expectations in order to return to the Caribbean in 1954 to found the Dominica Labour Party. A committed Fabian Socialist who worked indefatigably to uphold voting rights and safeguard the peasantry's participation in Dominican politics, she found herself expelled from the Party she had founded and excluded from island politics when the demands of black nationalism made it expedient. She found a place for herself in Dominican society, nonetheless, as a newspaper editor and spokesperson for the political opposition, roles that allowed her a lasting public life and through which she eked out a meagre living. She died in Roseau, Dominica, in 1986.

Towards the end of her life, as she pondered the choices she had made during her long political career, Allfrey came to regret her choice of politics over writing. "Politics ruined me for writing," she would muse wistfully when she despaired about having failed to earn the lasting legacy to which she aspired through her political work. It was at that juncture that she turned to the writing she had abandoned in favour of politics, struggling in the last few impoverished years of her life to see The Orchid House return to print for the first time since 1953, gather her scattered short stories into a book, reissue her four collections of poems, and finish In the Cabinet, the autobiographical novel about her years as a minister during the West Indies Federation, which she had started in 1961.

In all but the first of these goals she failed. She lived to see The Orchid House reissued in England in 1982 – a second American edition appeared in 1996 – but illness, poverty, and eventually death conspired against her efforts to claim her position as a pioneer among women writers in the Caribbean. In The Cabinet remained unfinished; her poems remain out of print. The best of her stories, many of which had appeared in the 1940s and 50s in English journals and newspapers such as Pan Africa, The Windmill, Argosy and the Manchester Guardian, are collected here for the first time. A handful have never been published before.

The 14 stories collected in this volume represent roughly a

third of the published texts and extant manuscripts found among Phyllis Shand Allfrey's papers. They are characteristic of the themes and techniques that distinguish her fiction, and, like her published and unpublished novels, have a strong autobiographical foundation. Allfrey wrote best about what she knew well – that which she had experienced herself or come to know first hand – and her subjects follow the trajectory of her peripatetic career. Every story connects, directly or indirectly, with an episode in her life – every text recalls a juncture in the path she followed from a childhood in the twilight of the British empire in the West Indies, through the voluntary exile that took her to the United States during the great depression and to England during the second world war, to a return to a West Indian social landscape transformed by struggles for labour reform, political independence, and federation.

Writing from a profound sense of her own West Indian identity, Allfrey centres her plots on the epiphanies that result from chance encounters between characters of different cultures, classes, outlooks, and – above all – races. As a writer, she was endlessly fascinated by the transformations brought about by juxtaposing perspectives that clashed – and occasionally crashed. These transformative encounters stem from affairs as mundane as the melodrama surrounding the naming of a new neighbourhood art centre – as in The Naming – where an artistic and lonely young man surrounded by working-class matrons finds his ideal of beauty in the self-portrait of a dead young woman with the unfortunate name of Mabs Boojoys. Or from the rapport that develops in Proserpeena and the Colonel between a Free-French colonel stranded in Dominica without an army during the second world war and the young servant woman who assembles a platoon of recruits for him from among the many Martinican refugees in Roseau. Rooted in Allfrey's confidence in common people's innate decency and fairness, they speak to the efficacy of facing the unfamiliar as instrumental in helping people rise above bigotry, narrow-mindedness and chauvinism.

In these tales Allfrey writes with light irony about the specificities of class, race, and gender relations in West Indian society. The delicate mockery of tone and wistful empathy that characterise her fictional renderings of the complexities of social life in Caribbean islands are her cultural legacy as a Dominican writer. Her ear attuned to the gentle satire and wry sense of the ridiculous that marks the Dominican character, she deploys them to bittersweet effect to unveil the intricate nuances of white mistress/black servant relations in O Stay and Hear, the absurdities of the strategies to prevent a marriage between a coloured baker and a scion of a white elite family in Uncle Rufus, and the poignancy of the lonely young protagonist of A Real Person, who despite the murder of his friend could still believe that "in spite of the mysterious and inexplicable conflict of faith and races in the world, it was still a world in which miracles happened."

Phyllis Shand Allfrey's short stories reveal a new dimension of a literary talent that was never allowed to reach full fruition. Subordinated as it always was to her political career, her published writing never reached in volume a level comparable to that of most West Indian writers of her generation. The stories collected here, however, by showcasing a new facet of her literary gifts and adding considerably to the sum of her known oeuvre, uphold her claim to a salient place in Caribbean literary history.

Lizabeth Paravisini-Gebert

O STAY AND HEAR

They are walking in the flower garden, and what are they singing? Something rather merry and mocking; the veering breeze blows up a few words now and then to the ears of a lady behind green bathroom blinds.

Now the lady raises a long pale arm and applies a little soap to it, at the same time peeping through the slats without rising from her cool bath water.

Samedi après-midi,
Madame-là tombait malade:
Voyez, cherchait l'Abbé...

The brown girls' arms are intertwined like snakes; yet somehow the plump hand of Melta, who is a maid by profession and fond of arranging flowers, reaches out with a sharp carving-knife and lops off half a bush of crimson roses between one stanza and another; both girls dip in a flying curtsy, and the thinner fingers of Ariadne, the eighteen-year-old cook, brush grass and come up with the dazzling spray.

Monsieur l'Abbé venait.
Il dit, Rome Saeculorum.
Madame-là comprend c'est 'rhum'.

But I thought they said the patois was common and that they disdained it, says this English Madame-là to herself, standing on a rush mat and dabbing off rivulets absently. To think of me, me myself, indulging in a cold bath at four o'clock in the afternoon! she comments inwardly.

When she told them about the sudden dinner, they had taken it very sweetly. "A business friend of the Master's." "Oh yes, Mistress: understood." "He is a director, but has quite a simple appetite." "Flying fish," says Ariadne. "And fried plantains," adds Melta.

"Oh no, I think not fried plantains – too hot. Something green. Perhaps a little stuffed avocado?"

"Stuffed with what, Mistress?" asks Ariadne bluntly.

"Oh, I don't know...perhaps some parsley?"

"The hen and the weeding boy have taken the parsley," Melta says.

"Then I leave it to you."

They are pleased: they like things being left to them. They take up the carving knife and go out into the garden. But instead of hunting for a last blade of parsley or a handful of chives, they dance around in the high soft breeze, lopping off roses. Their aprons lift and swirl, and they look like ballet dancers dressed as probationer nurses: the full skirts of their uniforms are covered with a flight of multicoloured wild ducks. Their little song has come to an end, so they begin it again:

Samedi après-midi,
Madame-là tombait malade...

It is Saturday afternoon; and if I had fainted in my bath I could have drowned, I could have died, and those girls wouldn't have been in the least concerned, thinks Madame-là anxiously. She is envious of them, because they have each other for gay company. Now they are advancing on the lonely house, using their bouquet to shoo before them a brown hen with well-clipped wings. This is the pullet, which had the temerity, in the middle of a sweltering West Indian summer, to lay one egg in a secret place and hatch out a solitary cream-coloured chicken.

The girls drive the hen, the hen cups the chick with her shortened wings, all rush in a giggling, clucking posse towards the kitchen steps, under which the hen and chicken disappear. Something about the hen and chick has a secret power of mirth over the girls: they sit on the bottom step, laps full of roses and arms round each other's necks, laughing fecklessly.

Madame-là has her own method of attracting attention: she leans out of the window with a small brass bell suspended on a string, and tinkles it above the white-capped heads.

"Melta! Ariadne! Don't forget Mr Whitborough is coming to dinner!"

"Yes, Mistress," says Melta in her deep, harsh contralto. "We forget ourselves. The hen makes us laugh."

But they are speaking to an empty window: Madame-là has

slipped downstairs to greet them on the landing. She wants to know what there is about the hen...

About the hen? Ariadne starts to laugh again. It is really intolerable. At last Melta says: "It is the hen and her child."

"The hen and her child is like ourselves," says Ariadne, rising to full copper height.

Melta is engaged in slicing off the rose stems, for all the world as if she is going to stuff Mr Whitborough's avocado pears with the trimmings. Madame-là notices how pretty both girls are, and that Ariadne is the one with the crisp, scornful upper lip.

"She takes pride in her chick, which is of a lighter complexion than herself," volunteers Melta.

"Just as we do," says Ariadne. They both laugh again, to see the amazement and appeal on Madame-là's face. It is giving them great pleasure to satisfy her curiosity tormentingly, bit by bit.

"I have a daughter, of very pale coloration," says Ariadne. "It is a girl. She is name Dolores."

"I also have a child, a boy name Ah-but-not. He is even so light as Adne's child, and born in the same month," says Melta.

"And how old are these children?" asks Madame-là, sounding lost. When she says the word "children" she looks wonderingly at their continuing childish arabesque against a background of roses.

"Two years at Epiphany," says Melta, and Ariadne echoes, "E-pi-phan-y."

"But where are they?"

"Where?" ask the girls together, astonished. "With our

mothers in the country, Mistress, naturally."

Ariadne declares, "We were raised up as neighbours. We do everything together."

Madame-là makes an effort, and collects herself. "You must bring the children to see me."

"Yes, Mistress." They undulate evasively.

"But don't forget the dinner. Perhaps I could arrange the roses, to save time?"

Melta lays down the stems reproachfully. To create a diversion, Ariadne exclaims with cunning: "I can hear the Master's step, Mistress."

So Madame-là goes back upstairs and finds that Rodney indeed stands, steaming with recent energetic action, on the upstairs veranda. A strange redness overlays his sun-browned face. "Have you been playing tennis?" she asks him.

"No, darling," says Rodney, turning his back to reveal that his shirt is torn to shreds. "I've been fighting."

All her life she has been wanting Rodney to be successful and masterful, and now she is not sure that success really suits him. Is he, after all, getting too tough?

"With the skipper of the Douce Hélène," he answers her question tersely.

"Oh Rodney! That poor black man!"

"He nearly made me two thousand pounds poorer, by tipping our new engine into the sea. I had practically to stun him to get it eased back into the boat until we could land it."

She is silent, envisaging the horrid scene, a large lump of tangled steel perilously rocking, and Rodney springing at the skipper's gleaming torso. But Rodney appears unconcerned:

he removes his shredded shirt and makes for the bathroom.

To soothe him further, she calls through the netted swing door: "I have a theory about the social aspects of... "

But Rodney calls back: "Oh lord, no theories! Not with Whitborough coming to dinner!"

She is hurt, because really her theory is quite delicate and distinguished. She believes now that people in this tropical island do not make love for romantic reasons, but as social and evolutionary means. She is thinking of Melta and Ariadne and their children of light coloration, and the hen and the chick; it all seems to link up.

Fastening her pearls above the surf-green voile, she sighs, and then she begins to hum the catchy little song the girls were singing in the garden; going downstairs a moment later to see how Mr Whitborough's dinner is progressing.

If there is any dinner at all, it must be incarcerated in the frightening iron oven. Even the open coal-pot has disappeared. So have the girls.

Madame-là runs back upstairs in distress. "Rodney! I can't find the maids – and the coal-pot has gone, too." She hunts for her little brass bell.

"Don't worry," he says. "They are probably ironing out each others' hair with flat-irons. They always do before a dinner-party. Look out of the back window and you'll see them at it."

He is quite right. Ariadne is stretched on a piece of sacking outside the maids' room; Melta is applying a sizzling iron to her short, crimped hair, pulling as she presses. It is a painful scene, like an operation, and is transforming the girl into a sophisticated Arawak.

"And I can't think," cries Madame-là, "why they should want to have hair as straight as ours, when they mock at us so!"

Rodney laughs. He goes to a cabinet and pours out two long frosted drinks, to fortify them against their guest.

Yet, after all, the evening turns out smooth and gracious. Mr Whitborough does most of the talking; as Rodney has hinted, he is a man of theories. He is a much-travelled man, and makes a good story of how he found an almost untarnished button of his glorious regiment on a high slope in the Himalayas. Once, too, he entered an African chieftain's hut and was surprised to see the pennant of his yacht club fluttering above a four-poster.

"Fluttering?" Madame-là cannot resist exclaiming, thinking of the draught on the dying chieftain – she having imagined African huts as windowless as igloos...

"But not the least charming of my adventures," says Mr Whitborough, over the crimson roses – he is quite handsome for his age, and his quivering nostrils seem to devour the flying fish before he lifts his fork... After all, the dinner is superb, though it seems to have been cooked in ten minutes, and the mysterious stuffing which inflates the yellow-green avocado pears must always remain a secret. "When I visited this island once, not so awfully long ago, my friend Arbuthnot and I went up the Rivière Fantasque: he was trying to net rare birds for his tropical aviary, and I was after edible crabs. We sat there on the river bank, enjoying the scene and contemplating a plunge, when suddenly – "

The memory is so sweet, so incomparable, that Mr Whitborough's nostrils meet his upper lip in an unusual smile.

"Suddenly there was this voice, coming from the depths of

what I can only describe as a jungle; and we saw that higher up the river two comely girls, clothed only in a series of patches, were beating some cloth against a rock in the water and singing. At least, one of them was singing: and I am sure you will never guess what the words were."

"A song about a sick lady on Saturday afternoon," Madame-là puts forward, startling Rodney by her sudden vivacity. She has taken advantage of Melta's absence with the emptied plates: but she knows, she is positive that behind the glazed screen two interlinked forms are panting against each other with suppressed giggles.

Mr Whitborough stares at Madame-là in astonishment.

"And how the Abbé was called in – " she starts to explain.

"Oh no!" Mr Whitborough states firmly, authoritatively. "Nothing as ribald as that. Something very strange, almost, one might say, moving. A Shakespearean song to an Elizabethan air. We distinctly heard it: O stay and hear, your true love's coming...and the other voice took it up: That can sing both high and low. I remember how it echoed down the valley. Both high and low. It quite put poor Arbuthnot off his game. He dropped the net, and three rare specimens escaped."

"That's a beautiful tale, Whitborough – one of your best," says Rodney.

"And the most beautiful thing is that it's quite true," says Mr Whitborough.

"I believe it," says Madame-là sparkling.

"But surely that's not the end of it?" says Rodney.

"Ah, my dear fellow," says Mr Whitborough, "I have learnt by long experience as a raconteur that there is a point at which one ends a story. That little tale has an element of pure, unexpected romance. To carry it further would be crude. Since you press me, Arbuthnot went up the river, after his birds or after the girls – I don't know which."

"And did you ever find any edible crabs?" asks Madame-là, borrowing an inflection of mockery from somewhere. She does not expect Mr Whitborough to reply; besides, Melta has just come in with a crystal bowl full of fruit jelly. The night is so hot that the bright, rainbow-coloured mound wobbles dangerously, on the brink of disintegration.

It looks as if it is shaking – shaking with secret laughter.

BREEZE

I was stretched out on a mat under the impenetrable mango tree in the back garden sucking pear drops and reading a very old copy of Tiger Tim's Weekly, for I had been told not to show myself at the front gates. Although innocent of any design on the reputation of the white official class, I was in disgrace.

My great-uncle, the colony's medical officer, had issued a statement to the press that the prevalent epidemic was kaffir-pox, a disease that was unlikely to afflict people of pure European blood. Unfortunately, the first white victim of this unpleasant ailment was the Anglican archdeacon and the second was myself, then a child of ten.

My nurse, finding me on that morning fretful and convalescent, had bribed me to stay out of sight under the mango tree by giving me a bag of sweets and making many promises which I knew she would not keep. My spotty face was spellbound over the English comic strips, and every now and then I would break one of my nurse's don'ts and scratch my legs with the hand that turned the pages and brushed away flies.

I must have been there for over half an hour before a heavy rustling in the boughs above me made me conscious that something larger than bird or animal was about to slide to the ground.

It was Breeze, Breeze the wild girl, the notorious creature, who had been studying me in silence, but could not bear to see the last pear drops vanish into my listless mouth. Leaping down like a panther, Breeze grabbed the bag and then, a pear-drop bulging out of her cheek, greeted me:

"Hullo skinny! Got the kaffir-pox?"

Although I had never met Breeze before and only seen her once in the distance being chased by a policeman, I knew who she was and a great deal about her. She was the girl who had no home, who lived wild, who was only fourteen, but had been to jail five times, who stole, who wore no clothes or at most one garment; yes, she looked exactly the way the elders said she did, crispy hair shaved, face hard and saucy and merry...and as if to demonstrate those legs which were as fleet as the wind and which had inspired her name, Breeze vaulted up into the branches again, her shapeless grey garment flapping.

"Oh, do you live in our mango tree, Breeze?" I exclaimed in admiration, ignoring Breeze's insulting behaviour, for having attained a high branch, she leaned down grinning like the Cheshire cat and calling out just loudly enough for me to hear:

"Skinny, skinny, poxy, poxy."

After a while I became irritated by these epithets and muttered back:

"Jail bird, jail bird. Naked jail bird."

"Like to see me naked? Like to see how I get out of this dress when they chase me?" asked Breeze, and I nodded avidly.

She slid down the trunk of the mango tree again, and with a single wriggle of her bronze shoulders disposed of the shapeless sack, which had a large neck opening and no buttons. She stood there before me in maidenly magnificence, and as if the sight of her was not sufficient to shame my puny child limbs, she remarked: "Wouldn't call me skinny, would you? That's my town clothes. When I live in forest I live free."

I gazed at her enviously. To live free! Wasn't that what every child desired! Not to be fretted on hot days by starched muslin dresses and cotton bloomers! To sleep in trees like a bird! And to be as beautiful a series of round shapes as Breeze, who was what the elders called ominously, "a Big Girl Now."

"Wish't I could be you, Breeze," I complained.

But Breeze said surprisingly, "Rather be skinny. Don't run so fast now I'm grown. They catch me. Wanted to put me to school. Want me to live on cooked food. Want to put me to work. Listen Skinny," she bent down and glared at me terrifyingly, her brown shining face very near, "know what the p'leece want me to be? Want me to be a bucket-lady."

Now although I was only ten I knew well that to be a bucket lady was to pursue one of the two most ignominious professions in the colony; the other being designated "huckster," and having something or other to do with meeting ships and trading with sailors.

"A bucket-lady!" I said aghast.

Breeze to empty our privy pail for one-and-sixpence a week or worse – the privy pail of some family of lower social standing! Breeze having to walk carefully with a stinking bucket poised on her turban, sneaking down the lesser streets where no white people lived, towards the sea-dump, on dark nights!

"Don't ever let them catch you and make you a bucket-lady, Breeze!" I cried.

"Oh, I don't mind smells, I sleep in closets on rainy nights," said Breeze proudly, "but I mind walking slow and not living free, I mind doing same things every week. Hey, what you got on your arm, poxy?" she exclaimed, seizing the wrist on which the tight little gold-coiled bracelet, a gift from my great-uncle when I was five, clung like a permanent handcuff.

"Gold! Real gold!" cried Breeze, her eyes greedy for the yellow shining thing. "Gimme that. Make me lovely earrings? I got pierced ears. Gimme, or I'll take it."

And as I crouched away from her, nor knowing whether to cry or to comply, Breeze made a nearer tiger leap and snarled in my ear: "You gimme. Take it off or I'll bite it off." While I huddled petrified and fascinated, she added: "And I'll bite your hand off, too."

Hastily, I tugged at the bracelet, trying to part its two thick gold knobs with my left hand; fortunately, I had grown so thin that it came away suddenly, leaving red marks on my wrist. It rolled on the grass and Breeze picked it up and put it in her mouth, where it gleamed like a bit between her ferociously beautiful teeth.

I began to howl with rage and loss, and Breeze, hearing a bustle in the building behind me, snatched up her grey dress and slipped naked into the undergrowth. Yet so strong was my fear of Breeze, and perhaps also my loyalty to her enviable freedom, that I lay howling on the grass with my wrist tucked under my stomach, refusing to say what was the matter.

I never saw Breeze again, and nobody ever found out what had become of my gold bracelet. I heard of her further escapades, of course, and would listen with fascinated horror to tales of how she bit a policeman and sent him to hospital for weeks, or how she kicked the matron over, jumped the prison wall and disappeared into the hills. While I listened to these anecdotes I would think of Breeze with fond partisanship.

After a while I also became "a Big Girl Now" and left the colony for the milder savagery of boarding school.

The other day I met an American captain at a cocktail party, and he told me how he had visited my colony just before the war to make watercolour sketches. He told me how when his ship pulled into the bay, a young woman carrying a tray full of terrible beads and junk, her face powdered till it looked blue, and her lips painted purple, stepped up the gangway, and oh boy! What a type! She was a walking tigress, and when she swept off that ship she took with her the chief petty officer and half a dozen sailors and a bribe of a pound from the purser to clear off and quit making a nuisance of herself, for it seemed that even the local police couldn't keep her in order. "Gee, she was a darn beautiful coloured woman, and I'd have given a lot to have seen her with her face washed and as nude as a diving boy."

THE OBJECTIVE

People keep asking me why my elder sister married the bishop, and I keep on telling them that she fell in love with him on a moonlight night in the tropics, and they don't believe a word of it, they simply don't believe me. The moonlight was so fierce that night that Cyril, our cock, began to crow immediately after dinner (this was nothing unusual; he always did it when the moon was full). I think it was Cyril who woke me up, because he suddenly got hoarse and stopped crowing, and what with the silence and the smell of jasmine outside my window, I could not sleep any longer. So I got up and went into Natalie's room. I surprised her in a pair of grey flannels and a yellow shirt, with one leg out of her window, which overlooked the low kitchen roof. She frowned at me and said crossly: "Alice, what are you doing at this time of night?" – quite as if it was a perfectly normal thing for her to be out the window in pants when the Catholic church bells chimed midnight austerely in the distance; treating me like a childish culprit, when she knew only too well that I was barely two years younger than herself. So I hung out my tongue and made a nasty eye at her, and she told me I needn't advertise that I was bilious.

"Well, whatever are you doing in Daddy's trousers?" I asked.

"Exploring."

"Oh! Do you do it often? May I come?"

"Not in that horrible nightgown," said Natalie.

"I'll take it off," said I, and did; a simple action, as the neck was very wide and slipped easily over my ribs and hips, which were equally prominent. I stood there in a triangle of silver, feeling naked and gawky. "You may have my purple bloomers," said Natalie kindly. I put on the bloomers and a pair of tennis shoes with no laces and a rust-coloured jersey.

"Before we set forth," said Natalie, changing into her sepulchral voice which was so thrilling, "I must tell you my objective."

"Oh! Do you always have an objective?"

"This is my first," said Natalie, "we have a delicate engagement ahead. You will have to carry the lantern. I'll take the torch. I made a bet with myself."

She paused. She was always making bets with herself, and she faithfully carried out either the penalty or the reward. You would find her giving up cake out of the Lenten season, and at the same time buying ginger beer for three nights running, on account of a mysterious bet. It was a great honour to be let into one of her bets.

"I bet," said Natalie, pleased with my silence, "that the new bishop will be bald. You know Daddy and Mother would not let us go down to the jetty with the reception, because they said we needed sleep and the ship was late. So I bet. I bet that he was bald, and I swore that I'd find out for myself tonight. And here I go. Follow me!"

She put the rusty hurricane lantern into my hands, and crying "No time to lose!" she vaulted out the window onto the roof below. I knew better than to express amazement or lag behind. In a moment I too had dropped down and scrambled into the back garden. We unlatched the wooden gate and slipped by the hedges in silence. "Slink along," growled Natalie once; but slinking was really unnecessary, as everybody had gone to bed; people did not loiter in the moonlight, not in this tropical island, unless there was a party, or a lover to meet, or someone was dead. Even the police went to bed.

We heard a lot of noises, but they were all quite natural: swishing of palms, the soft crash of the sea before it sucked out through the stones again, a few cocks crowing here and there, and the thud of ripe fruit falling. It did not take us long to slink into the bishop's grounds. There was an empty sentry box standing by the gate, for the bishop's palace had once been the fort. We slunk past it and through the shrubbery to the walls of the old military building. In the big bedroom (we knew all the rooms well, for we had played games in them while they were being done over), there burned a dim lemon light. It occurred to me to ask Natalie how she would have found out the condition of the bishop's scalp had the room been dark. She was very short with me, and asked me what I thought the torch was for. We pressed close to the rough stone wall and listened, holding our breath.

"Now this is where you come in useful," said Natalie in her most subtle whisper. "Bend down and let me climb on your shoulder so that I can peep in, and after that you can have a turn." I obediently squatted on the ground. The bishop's bedroom was on the ground floor, in fact the fort was nothing more than an antique bungalow, and everything was apparently easy. But heaving Natalie up to the rim of the windowsill was hard work. She weighed a lot, and I was smitten with envy because her behind was getting so round and fashionable. I sighed, and nearly toppled her forward; but she pressed her hands against the wall, and we achieved it.

Of course I could not whisper to Natalie while she was sitting on my neck. And she could not tell me what she was seeing, but in less than a minute she was kicking me wildly in the ribs, and I knew she was dying to laugh or something, so I bent over and let her fall off with a loud flop. She picked herself up, grabbed me frantically by the hands, and dragged me away through the shrubs. Just before we reached the sentry box she rolled on the ground, giggling and gasping. I felt rather cold towards her. "What about my turn, Natalie?" I asked heavily.

"He smiled at me," said Natalie, ignoring my tone.

I forgot to be angry. "And his hair . . . ?"

"Oh, that!" said Natalie in her most lofty, her most irritating, her most dreamy voice, "Certainly he wasn't bald. Of course I lost my bet. He is young, that is, young for a bishop. And very handsome. He was reading a book in bed. Such a distinguished man! Far more distinguished than the governor. I could easily, yes, easily, fall in love with him."

"But bishops always have wives," I said.

"I bet this one doesn't have a wife," said Natalie. "I bet I am the first really beautiful girl he has ever seen, and that is why he smiled. I bet I'll marry the bishop by the time I am twenty-one."

"Wait a minute," I said, because I was hardly able to bear Natalie's triumph, not having seen the bishop, having been done out of my fun. "Remember you bet he would be bald. You lost."

"That is a mere nothing," said Natalie. "The penalty is that you and I have to catch thirteen mole crickets on the tennis court before we go back to bed."

So Natalie and I caught mole crickets until three in the morning. I did not feel that I was wasting time, because the mole crickets were chewing up the lawn, and I liked to play tennis on even ground. But the little devils were hard to catch. We baited them with the lantern and a sheet on a pole, and the moon was so bright, they wouldn't rise. Natalie put them in a jam pot and kept them in her bedroom.

Next Sunday we went to the cathedral to hear the bishop preach. We heard him preach every Sunday for four years, but I never felt that I knew him really well, and gradually the ladies of the parish came round to the same conclusion too. Anyhow, my sister Natalie married the bishop when she was twenty.

PARKS

Now that she was sitting in Central Park, wrapped in furs, looking very beautiful, as always…now that she watched with reminiscent eyes the antics of her baby girl in oozing March snow…now that her car was due to call for them in half-an-hour…she brooded, almost with complacence, on the memory of that other park.

No, not quite complacently. Central Park, straggled with ugly young men, helpless nursemaids and darling children, was nearly calm; and beyond its low stone wall New York City flowed like a river of unrest, remote. But the other garden, the tropical one! Its solitary beauty had been too forcibly vivid for complacence. The green of it hurt; the trees wavered like tremulous lips. It had been, in alternation, gaudy and uncompromisingly sombre.

To the seated woman, her life, with all its implications and absurdities, seemed at the moment to be one ghastly sham. She was harking back to her infancy and childhood, to the afternoons when her mother had dragged her to a bench under the velvet tamarind tree. There they had sat and discussed white people, who were so evil and vulgar and irritatingly immaculate. Her dead father had been included in the contemptuous summary. He had given Minta Farrar her curious fairness, her tawny-crinkled hair; but it was from her mother that she inherited the large, burning eyes now gazing at the slope over which the Pilgrim Fathers' statue presides.

Minta's father had been a drunken Irishman, her mother, a seamstress, exactly one-fourth African. She had been born in the hush before a terrific September hurricane, which had ravaged the island of Dominica in the British West Indies. She was now twenty-seven years of age, married to a wealthy American who had an office "downtown" and a coarse sense of humour, and now she was white…spotless…retrieved, in the eyes of her present world. She wore furs and sat in Central Park.

Hers had been an extraordinary evolution, occasioned through her mother's surrender of her child to a philanthropist from America who had considered adoption of a lovely hybrid oddly worthwhile. From that time onwards her days had been a series of adjustments and smothered resentments.

How to trace her evolution as she did, while she watched her child squelch with little squeaks and gurgles up and down the snowy incline? There were so many gaps, so many sordid particulars. It is easy to picture her being promenaded in the tropical park by an almost fanatical parent, but hard to see her growing slowly, slowly in brain and form, growing away from her mother just the degree that lay between them – growing towards the white, leaving a great gulf fixed between that pale coffee colour and her own ivory.

Now, she would not force herself to summarise the dull school years, when her whole instinct of warm languor had revolted against tuition. She sighed, and endeavoured to shake off the mood of introspection. But no, the brooding clung: her mind turned again to the shade of the velvet tamarind tree.

Mason, the new English chauffeur, respectfully addressed Minta from a few yards' distance. The car was waiting near the 72nd Street entrance. He had seen Mr Farrar off to Boston in the 4:10 train. Was Mrs Farrar ready?

Minta stared at him vaguely for a second, her eyes dumb and dark. A quick thought stung her: Mason, in the island of Dominica you would be a third-rate planter, perhaps, and I…a social outcast. I should crave a smile from you, be grateful for the least gesture of desire. And here…you are my servant. Funny, isn't it, Mason?

"Yes, please, Mason."

At home in the expensive Park Avenue apartment, the child was fretful. She was a capricious little thing, endowed (her mother imagined) with some degree of her own obstinacy. The small, wayward creature turned from Minta and stormed into her nurse's arms, so Minta left the nursery and went slowly down the passage to her bedroom.

She sat before her mirror and shook her hair free. Never long, it brushed her shoulder like lovely pale fibre. Save for its colour, it was telltale hair. Thank heaven, the child had not a single telltale feature; the child would never be a suspect.

Minta thought: I am a woman in a sad predicament. I have a husband, but I do not love him. I have a child who does not need me; I have too much money and no friends...I am afraid of friends. I am sad, and obliged to be ashamed of my sadness.

She undressed, slipped on a wrapper, and dismissed a hovering maid with the injunction that she was not to be disturbed, not even for dinner. Then she lay on her bed. Everything seemed to lapse and grow dim.

Her torpor was dangerous. She lay there for some hours until it became unbearable, like a sense of doom. Then she remembered something that she had been told several months ago, laughingly, about a certain night club in Harlem. She had never been brave enough to discover it for herself. But tonight was the night for bravery.

Tonight Minta was the Lady of Shalott, in very truth. She rose, flung her torpor from her valiantly, knelt and unlocked her special private chest wherein lay hidden belongings seldom touched, never viewed by other eyes. Her mother's photograph and illegible letters lay there, on the top. These Minta Farrar did not scrutinise. She flung the wrapper from her, as she had discarded her torpor, and robed herself in her treasure costume: the costume of a native West Indian belle.

The long mirror revealed her lovely self, revealed the full gown with its trailing back, the brilliant silk foulard neckpiece, heavy gold earrings, gorgeous turban.

Now Minta's eyes were very bright. She added red to her lips. Her nostrils quivered a little. The turban hid her hair. Into a deep side pocket she thrust some notes and the key to her apartment. After tucking her train into the narrow waistband she drew on her evening cloak, went out, and hailed a taxi. Poised there in the frozen darkness, she was indeed Tennyson's fated Lady, about to cast herself into the river of unrest.

"The Trinidad Nightclub, Harlem," she ordered, quoting number and street.

The taxi-driver shot uptown along Park Avenue and then branched off to Fifth Avenue, grinding to a standstill when the traffic lights of New York flared red against him. He was not disposed to marvel that a lady of this sort should wish to penetrate the notorious and amazing haunt of the negro race. At length he opened the door, received his due and something more, saw the lady into the nightclub. From the street the place appeared stolid, almost respectable. The main entrance was very narrow.

Minta knew she was defying the gods. She was mad. She, so fortunate, so secure of her kind! Her kind…ah, there was the urge, the tragedy; these were her people. In most cases the sensitive coloured outcast strains toward the white race. But Minta yearned for humble brown companionship.

She allayed her suspicions of the doorkeeper, entered and looked around, a nervous little smile on her lips.

A Barbadian mulatto, splendidly handsome, smiled directly at her with gleaming teeth…hesitated…smiled again, swung her into his clasp. Immediately they were dancing.

At first they danced in silence, their bodies in glorious rhythm. Then they talked softly, addressing each other by their naturally proffered Christian names. They said to each other that they were homesick. Terribly homesick.

"Minta, I'm sure dead anxious to get back," the Barbadian said, in his inimitable accent.

"Me, too," she breathed wistfully. "To be really warm again, and suck oranges in the sunlight…"

"And mangoes," he added, pleased with the thought. "Don't forget the mangoes; suck 'em until your face is yaller…"

How incomparably friendly and comforting the Barbadian was! He asked her no questions, for hers was the kind of quiet beauty, which stills curiosity. But he told her, very simply, quite a lot about himself. He was an apprentice to an undertaker, and worked in a little black hole of a place where, in the winter, everything seemed cold and dirty. He came to the Trinidad Nightclub on Saturday nights to find gaiety, to forget himself as much as possible. At this place he spent his small earnings, sometimes became uproariously drunk. He had no kindred in the United States, simply one or two casual and vagrant friends.

Their nostalgia was their bond and their escape. Around them swayed masses of West Indian inebriates; and there seemed to Minta to be a sort of dark splendour in the revelry. The women were all in costume…the men, in varying garbs, were all drunk, or worse…except Minta's Barbadian, who was intoxicated by the anodyne of the lovely, sad woman in his arms. He sensed mystery about her, was gentle and almost courteous. He thought that perhaps she was rich, had a white lover; she was so nearly white. He was infinitely pitiful. She was from Dominica, she was beautiful, she was homesick.

The band broke into a queer West Indian melody – a "paseo"

dance with its long, lilting steps and puzzling time-beats. In a corner the notorious Smash-Nose Stevens, a Jamaican, made a slight disturbance about a timid brown girl who cowered behind a southern negro from New Orleans. Somewhere in the middle of the room husky voices sang the words of the "paseo", half in Creole English, half in French Patois.

I love you awready,
Moi aimé 'ous déjà…

The Barbadian sensed that his partner could not see the repulsive aspect of the huddled room. She was lost in some peculiar dream of her own. For himself, he was hardened to this ribaldry. He liked it, on the whole. But his lady, his Dominican Minta, liked it for an unknown quality that was unreal and delicate.

Instead of surging to the bar with the crowd they had discovered a table isolated from the cabaret and there had eaten, like two greedy children. Minta glanced into his eyes while they ate and fancied instantly that his emotion was the same as hers, hardly cognisant…and why? Because they fitted, they understood! How suddenly two personalities can be riveted – bound by a glance, by a sharing of environment, by a gorgeous alikeness! Naively critical, they studied each other and perceived their semblance in a flash. But they were afraid of the ephemeral nature of their recognition.

Minta afterwards remembered little of the incidental detail of that evening. She only remembered that it had seemed warm, and full of her own people, and noisy with the crash of West Indian music, and vivid with coloured lights and careless laughter. She remembered the Barbadian's last words of encouragement as he handed her into a yellow taxi:

"Luck to you, Minta. Moi aimé 'ous déjà!"

She remembered nothing else save her dazed disrobing. Yet she had swallowed less than a glassful of some familiar drink. Perhaps hers was the blank mind of one who has sought wild danger and discovered fellowship.

In the late morning she was very tired. Still some ghost of that dark gloom hung over her.

The maid came in, drew the curtains, and stooped to pick up the disarray of bright silks on the floor. Minta waved her away: "No, no. Leave them there, please."

The child came in, running...climbed on the bed; was wriggling off again when a shiny earring lying on the bedspread arrested her. She snatched it up and tugged at the swinging, pear-shaped drops. Minta was angry – strangely angry.

"Give it to me," she said, taking it from the baby's little hand. "It is not for you. You must never, never have anything like that. That is mother's, see?"

The baby wailed, was extricated from her mother's grip.

"I'll take her out to the park," said the nurse. The woman's voice was a gesture of resignation, for it was Sunday morning and she was a good Catholic.

"Oh, very well," Minta replied, suddenly hopeless. Yes, take the child to Central Park. But the other park...ah, oranges, and mangoes...There is a difference.

Her sorrow was that she would always know the difference, would always hunger.

But now there was something to be done. She would make up a parcel and address it to the little undertaker's hovel in Harlem. That parcel would contain the treasured costume, the turban, the foulard neckpiece, and the gold earrings. Some day, perhaps, he would give them to a comfortable brown love, and together the happy two might guess at their significance. The money she had thrust into a pocket last night would await his astonished hand; next Saturday he could go to the Trinidad Nightclub and make himself richly drunk.

For herself, she would have a bath and some breakfast.

LETTER TO
A GERMAN-AMERICAN LAUNDRESS

Mrs Brieger, you remember when you came to us the first time, how you asked us whether we were real-born English or whether we got our voices from school-learning? And when we said that we were real-born English, you said that'll be fifty cents less the week; and afterwards we found out that you lowered the price, not because you liked the English, but because people who got their voices from foreign school-learning were always richer than the other kind.

So right at the start, Mrs Brieger, we began to like you and to have a respect for your sense of proportion. That winter was a very hard one for us, and you dropped twenty-five cents more off the bill every now and then, so's one of you folks can go to a movie and not notice the difference.

After that we grew interested in your private life, and began to ask questions.

You told us that you were sorry about your goitre; you knew it had a bad look to a new customer, but it wasn't catching. It came from not eating enough seafood, and the poor water of the district.

Come to think of it, you said, laundresses generally have goitres anyway. They get a crick in the neck stooping over the tubs.

Have you been a laundress long, Mrs Brieger?

Well, I was one for 16 years and then my son grew up and I leaned on him to support me. (I'd been a widow a long while.) Henry was a good boy, nothing that you could complain about, and when he took him a wife we all moved into a new place together. And then come the babies. But Henry had a good job over to the Chevrolet plant. So we didn't live too mean, and Doris she always had the babies at home, quite cheap. But they was all boys; and she keep right on trying for a girl, so she could doll it up. You never saw such a one, always in the beauty-parlour if she had a nickel. Then depression hit us. She had the three youngsters, yes, and the pity was that they was all boys. Or she might have stopped.

Did Henry lose his job, then?

Now you guessed right the first time. He did; and I had to go back to the old tubs again. But I'd been keeping in practice anyway, doing up the kids' clothes. We liked to see them looking nice. You wouldn't think of it now, seeing them in their patches. But my, they had their two-three linen shirts and pants a week, summers, and in the winter the cutest little man-tailored woollens. We had to tighten down, after a while; for since Henry was out of work, Doris had Donald and Kenneth.

You are a wonderful woman, Mrs Brieger.

Now what would you do if you had a son and he looked to you for help in a hard time. Would you let him starve?

We didn't mean Henry. We were thinking of Doris and all the boys. We don't know how you had the patience.

You got parents over in Europe, haven't you? Now, say you was to walk right in there with a baby of your own, with two, three, four or five babies, I'm telling you they'd be that glad to see you they'd never let you out of the house again, even if they had to sell the old cow-pasture and go to work for the Jews to keep you. There's such a feeling you get, when you see those little creatures opening up their eyes to look at the world, and you know they'll likely be looking at the world long after you've passed out of it, and that they're all you can leave behind of yourself, that's the way a grandmother feels in particular.

Maybe all grandmothers don't feel the same, Mrs Brieger.

Them that don't, they shouldn't have been parents in the first place. I'm telling you, Doris is set to have another one by . the end of the summer, and the pity is that it isn't yours, for you're a good-looking pair of young people. But you'll be having your own soon, I feel sure. (No you can't kid me, not for long.) Anyway, when I'm doing my rinsing down cellar and I feel pretty weak, I could turn Doris out for the trouble she gives me, and she not doing a stroke of work other than cook wieners every so often, and stuff herself with them. But I know that when I see the little thing I'll be buying it a new buggy out of my savings, for the old buggy is just about wore out.

That wasn't the only time you lingered to talk to us, Mrs

Brieger. In the end your talks became longer and longer, so that we always had a cup of coffee and some cake ready on laundry days. We bet you a dollar that Doris's new baby would be a girl, and you bet us one week's washing that ours would be a boy. One day you brought Doris's little girl to see our little boy, and we paid our bets. You put your granddaughter on the bed beside our Anthony; she was all dressed up in thick knitted clothes, but Anthony's tiny feet were bare, and you lectured us for not keeping him warm enough, and apologised for Dorothea's cradle-cap, but her mother always put her to sleep in a bonnet, and didn't grease her head.

Anthony and Dorothea never looked at each other once, and never made a sound, but lay there kicking.

That was near Christmas, you remember, and we told you that we were homesick for that damp little island called England where so many people lived and so many important things were always about to happen. You encouraged us, and advised us to go back there. Now I won't say that it was because of your encouragement and advice that we did go; but it is true that your words sounded wiser than any we had heard for a long time, and that they kept on echoing.

It's always a terrible thing, you said, to put an ocean between blood and blood, especially at Christmas time and birthdays and sickness and so on. There's no telling when death will come to the best of us. Now, as soon as you folks have gotten over paying for this baby here, and have saved up the price of an ocean-ride, it's my belief that you should make that trip and settle down in your own land. It's always a puzzle to me what you do with your weekends. Just sit home and read the paper, I suppose. Now this boy here, he needs the grandparents' house and garden you spoke about. I give him a year to find his feet, before he'll be asking for green grass instead of these boards...

We laughed, you remember, but now we wonder if we didn't begin to lay our plans with that laugh. Because very soon afterwards we started to prepare for the voyage. It took us a long time to save up, as things kept going wrong, but at last it happened. The last two months were the longest.

The night before the ship docked we were so gay, we drank whisky straight in the third-class lounge when Anthony was asleep. We won't pretend that we thought of you then in the least, Mrs Brieger. We were too excited.

Now I have to give you a great surprise, and tell you something, which will shock you terribly. For it seems that in those few years that we were away the grandparents had forgotten how to love children. They had put all the young birds out of the nest, and they found the nest just big enough for themselves. Instead of the children, a butler and a cook and a gardener and a scullery-maid had crept in. There was no room for us and no room for Anthony.

You would have thought that the pity of it was that we did not notice it right away. We were so dumb. We went up to the grandmother's room and showed her the baby. Then we did think of you, Mrs Brieger, when we saw her lying there under the silken eiderdowns cherishing the memory of her operations, cherishing her soft shapeless body that had ceased to be of service to the world and to anyone. Cherishing her body, while her heart had wasted away so small that it was a mere shrivel under the quilts, and all the love in it was for a child who had died long ago. And around her the crucifixes, for she was religious in the way of an Anglo-Catholic (which is a very funny way, Mrs Brieger). And standing by her the old gentleman, like a shadow waiting upon her whim. And Anthony was crying in my arms, because he was tired and perhaps also because he saw there the nothingness which you would have seen. We thought of you, Mrs Brieger, simply because you too had been ill and nobody had ever cherished you, and all the while you had been brave and loving.

Now after we had unpacked all our clothes, and made as if to pay a visit to good friends, and Anthony kept right on crying in his worst voice, then the knowledge came to us of what we had renounced by going away to America; that they had forgotten, and that they did not want us any more. I think it came the next morning, when we opened our eyes and saw out of the window the low blue English skies, heavy with clouds, so low that they pressed down upon us; and when we heard the birds singing more richly than any birds you've ever heard near Buffalo, New York, I quite assure you, Mrs Brieger. The smell of the garden came in, and it was beautiful and damp and flowery, and everything was beautiful, but just the same there was a feeling that it had all gone wrong and that there was no place for us. And Anthony kept right on crying in misery.

The butler came in with our tea, and we saw his pale brown hand setting it on the table, and saw his pale face with the fixed sneer on it, and we thought of how valuable he was to the grandparents and how valueless Anthony was, since they were not measuring life by its heart and its blood but by the little comforts of day to day, by early-morning tea and fires laid in the winter, by calling-cards and a nice front for the neighbours.

And so we could not stay, Mrs Brieger, more than a few days, because it grew worse and worse and a lump came in our throats, and the lovely damp smell of the garden turned rotten, and the voices of birds became the twitter of English voices, full of emptiness and incomprehension.

I am ashamed to write you these things, as you believe in kindness and generosity and grandmothers; but I had to write to you from us both, to say that we've adopted you for our grandmother, if you don't mind having us on top of all you've got already. Take care of your goitre and don't let Doris have any more babies. We'll buy you the golden locket you wanted for Dorothea with her name engraved, and you can take it off the laundry bill when we come back.

PROSERPEENA AND THE COLONEL

The room may have been a convent bedroom for a demoiselle save for an echo of subdued wildness. Colonel Gilet was conscious of incongruity when he laid his cap on the dressing table to mark proprietorship. Under the dressing table the paint had been kicked off by a young girl who had sat on a stool and swung her feet while dragging at tangled hair, and on the bookcase a few worn books leaned rakishly against each other. The bed cover was of nursery vintage: there were no pictures, but there were marks on the walls where things had been pasted on and scratched off again. And the views from the three windows, all startlingly different, were enough to make any young girl, or even a French colonel, dream. For the right-hand window gave on to mountains; the middle one seduced the eye downward to a mass of gilded and rosy flowers; and the third, which was in the middle of the northern wall and quite large, overlooked a courtyard with various outbuildings and a sort of well from which protruded a water tap, near which stood an empty monkey-house with a listless chain dangling in memoriam.

The Colonel saw that Proserpeena, having tipped down the luggage, had no intention of leaving him and he said to her after a little reflection: "You have the French Patois?" "Yes, sir," she replied in English. "Ah…" he pondered. "So you have perhaps friends in Martinique and Guadeloupe?" But Proserpeena shook her head. How should she know as yet whether he was a man of Vichy or a Gaulliste? The uniform meant little to her. She would give nothing away, and least of all Lou-Lou who had escaped and was now doing business by plying a rowboat to pick up refugees in the channels.

"I expect to be here for some time," said the Colonel, sighing a little as if in disappointment, for he guessed that Proserpeena's head was full of pregnant thought as she stood silently there; only he could not guess that she was hearing the voice of Miss Caroline. "…and Proserpeena, you will be the zombie and put misery on any guests we don't like, bring in a land crab and a couple of geckos and some grass full of betes-rouges and make things hot for them so that they leave at once…" Raising her lashes she looked dubiously at the Colonel. (It was Lou-Lou and not Miss Caroline who had told her of the terrible difference between the Gaullistes and the men of Vichy; yet Proserpeena linked up the Vichyites with Miss Caroline's natural enemies, by instinct.)

"And where do I wash?" asked the Colonel, who had noticed that the china basin was turned upside down and used as a base for a potted fern.

"Miss Caroline never washed in here. She said it wasn't civilised," said Proserpeena loftily. "She washed in the yard, so that she could talk to her monkey; or more privately, in the bathroom." Downstairs they went again, and he found himself in one of the outhouses, cool and dank as a stalactitic cave, perpetually and faintly dripping with running water from some leak or other, the large square stone bath like a miniature swimming pool lined with new greenish moss, coconut matting on the red-tiled floor. He turned on the shower and put his lean head under it; he liked the smell of verbena soap and the fresh old-linen towel Proserpeena had provided. While he was so engaged Proserpeena had darted out of the wide courtyard gate and passed a lightning verbal message to one of her best friends (she had so many best friends in the kitchen alley that she was never at a loss for a courier): "Tell Lou-Lou…"

The military gentlemen were in a hurry. They ate their lunch quickly and departed to Government Office on official business. Clothilde folded her hands over her stomach, groaned and lay down in the kitchen with her head on a sack of sweet potatoes.

Proserpeena helped Clothilde's daughter to wash the dishes expeditiously, then gave the little girl a syrup tablette to run away with. Madame and Miss Lyddie, exhausted by their hospitable efforts, were lying down in their rooms with the blinds drawn. Proserpeena went to the alley gate, detached the bell, and admitted Lou-Lou. Their bare feet made hardly a whisper as they padded upstairs to the Colonel's room, where Lou-Lou made an examination of everything that his clever fingers could unlock.

"He's taken the important papers with him," said Lou-Lou to Proserpeena in Martinique patois, which sounded elegant and Parisian to her ears. "But never mind. We don't want military secrets yet. We want to know where he stands, that's all." He wore on his near-black face a determined expression. Proserpeena adored him because he was sure and devoid of submissiveness: he could never forget that his island had provided France with a coloured General. "If *ce type* is a true man of France," he said, darting through the paraphernalia, the badges, the pamphlets dextrously, "I will go to High Mass with you on Sunday."

At last he was finished, and satisfied. He put everything back with scrupulous care. "Have we time...? he asked Proserpeena with his desiring eyes, with his lips, but Proserpeena said, smoothing the nursery bedspread: "No. We don't know their habits. These officers very seldom sleep in their chairs in the afternoon."

At dinner Miss Lyddie said: "The moon is rising. It's a lovely night. We might sit on the lawn after coffee, don't you think? Or will the mosquitoes trouble you?" But the officers were exchanging a few words. It was really admirable how Major Loome had all the earmarks, the positiveness of a superior officer. But of course poor Colonel Gilet was without a country, without a real command. He seemed to defer to the Major, he was a very modest man. Miss Lyddie preferred officers who were a little more authoritative.

Major Loome returned to the subject of education and his son. "Slacked a bit during his last year at Uppingham," he finished up. "Ah, we nearly sent my nephew to..." said Miss

Lyddie. "But of course...the money spent on his sister...rambling around Europe... I don't myself hold with over-educating girls...it seems to make them difficult, very difficult..."

"My daughter was also difficult, very difficult..." said the Colonel to Madame in a low voice.

"...Such different types of friends," went on Miss Lyddie. "My nephew always kept up with such charming people, people who would write us letters saying what delightful manners he had, but Caroline..."

The Colonel was thinking of the books in his borrowed bedroom. Hans Andersen, DH Lawrence, a life of Rosa Luxemburg, Bevis' The Story Of A Boy, and other volumes strange in juxtaposition. "And Proserpeena," he reflected.

They were walking in the moonlight, Miss Lyddie with Major Loome, well out of earshot, Madame and Colonel Gilet. "She doesn't write," said Madame mournfully. "They cannot write," said the Colonel; and they walked on in sorrowful silence. So deep was their silence and so deep the thick silver moonlight that the Colonel felt it coming over him again – the twinge, the uneasy, unaccountable silence. Here he was, in the middle of a war, he a retired country gentleman cruelly parted from his family, walking in uniform beside an aging lady in a tropical garden, and he was overcome by the enchantment of life. But now they had made a full circle and Miss Lyddie and the Major were facing them. "And I was just saying to the Major," said Miss Lyddie, "that your refugees have stolen all our island pigs and most of our chickens..."

The Colonel made his polite goodnights and went up to

Miss Caroline's room. He stood looking out of each window in turn. He could feel beauty intensely, he could feel a watchfulness around him; he was no longer happy. On his face was the borrowed expression of a man of affairs occupied with the problems of assembly and co-ordination.

A gallant company of stars escorted the Southern Cross, and enormous fireflies were swishing like meteors over the summerhouses. As the Colonel stood drinking in the surprises of tropical midnight, stretching his stiff limbs, he had another unexpected sensation: he could hear his own heart beating. He had lately thought that his sentimental heart had become atrophied with long waiting. But here in this place...and especially in this room...why, it was throbbing like a negro drum at carnival season! So I'm still a human being, said the Colonel, forgetting while he undressed to worry about his insomnia.

The Colonel slept. He even dreamed: and his dream was so strange that he would have hesitated to describe it save to a psychologist. For out of the stupor of sleep someone rose from Miss Caroline's narrow bed, and that someone, whose heart beat as his own, was a girl. She swung herself over the windowsill and dropped through clouds of wisteria into the crook of the sweet-lime tree, then into the oleander bushes where another and darker shape waited, whistling softly. The two girls joined hands and seemed to float across the lawn and pass through a dim hibiscus hedge with trumpet-shaped flowers. Everywhere the girls went the Colonel's heartbeat went with them like a drum, like their footsteps, exploring all the secret and wonderful places of the island: the caves where illicit rum was distilled; the old obeah women telling their tales with a Tim-tim, bois sec; the nutmeg groves haunted by ardent lovers; the forbidden swimming pools. Those mysterious girls and the Colonel's beating heart became part of the curving moon-and-starlit island, part of the thudding waterfalls and surf, the essence of life and daring and dream.

Early next morning Proserpeena brought him a cup of fresh-ground coffee and an orange. "Will you have the bath before the Major and the ladies get it?" she coaxed (but why did he think that she was coaxing him, almost commanding him?). He drank the coffee quickly and ate the orange while he floated in the bath, afterwards putting the peel in the pocket of his non-crush silk dressing-gown which the lady in New York had given him. No one else was stirring; he could tell by the coolness and the pale sky that it was very early indeed. He dressed and went down to the veranda, where Proserpeena very soon brought him a tray loaded with the most exotic breakfast he had ever tasted, even in Martinique.

It was while he sat smoking his first cigarette, musing on his difficulties and listening to the sounds of other risers in bedrooms above, that the gate clanked and Proserpeena dashed up the drive, gravel flying before her, to greet the ragged army led by Lou-Lou: a small regiment of dark-skinned French citizens, wearing clothes borrowed or stolen: coloured boys and men of all ages and sizes, their only arms sticks and cudgels, leafy branches and even palm-fronds. A tricolour made of two women's skirts and a sheet floated before them.

The Colonel rose. (They were forming ranks, amateurishly

but bravely, on the lawn; they were trying not to laugh and shout in their pride and excitement.) Miss Lyddie and the Major poked heads out of their bedroom windows simultaneously; and a moment later Madame appeared to share the extraordinary sight. When the coloured maquis had assembled they were a formidable crowd some four hundred strong. The Colonel marched forward to greet them with stern joy and dignity in his bearing.

"Vive la France! Vive la Martinique, Vive la Guadeloupe! Vive De Gaulle!" the throaty tempestuous voices cried, and the Colonel saluted. Then he took command of his men; he inspected them; he rapped out orders.

Miss Lyddie was grieved that the Major was only half-shaved and still in his shirt, but was proud to see that his expression betrayed pleasure and admiration and not chagrin. A "true sporting Englishman," she murmured.

The Colonel was making a little address to his men. He was speaking in clear slow French so that Madame, Miss Lyddie and the Major could enjoy the import. "…And I ask you, my compatriots, to remember that we are guests in this island and that I shall look with grave displeasure on any disorderly behaviour. For example, the removal of pigs and chickens…I intend to take disciplinary action…the appropriation of clothing…as regular soldiers, you must be prepared to enter barracks and not to sleep partout…"

Lou-Lou and certain of the younger men began to look disturbed, but the speech ended suddenly with a reference to the great duties of liberation, and Colonel Gilet, dismissing the assembly, smiled broadly and came forward to take each man's right hand in both of his, asking his name and congratulating him on his loyalty in the name of France. Clothilde, who was standing in the shade of a summerhouse with her daughter, observed sourly, "Well, a Colonel's no good without an army, is he? So our Lou-Lou had to fetch him one."

But where was Proserpeena? The Colonel, flushed to his high gaunt cheekbones, looked around for his dark angel, and met instead the eyes of Madame, lowered temporarily from their contemplation of the mountains and their dreams of lost children. Proserpeena was nowhere to be seen; for at that moment she was engaged in transporting the precious and forbidden Crown Derby vase to Miss Caroline's room, loaded with a tricolour bouquet of frangipani, plumbago and hibiscus. Carefully she danced over to the upturned china basin and removed the potted fern. Placing her floral tribute on the basin as on an altar, she stood away from it with her arms curved, a copper ballet dancer in a trance of hope or reverence or reminiscence.

UNCLE RUFUS

When I read those terrible words, I thought at once of Uncle Rufus. You may wonder why I thought of him first, when the letter was from my aunt, and the last paragraph said: "For two weeks now we have not had a single slice of bread – there is none to buy. Our people stand looking out to the horizon, searching for the ships, which are always overdue. When there is meat, the police are called out to control the queues, which are often violent. We are eating sliced breadfruit with every meal, and pray that it will never go out of season. The ground is rotten with the oranges, which cannot be exported. No doubt those in England still think of us as the islands of sunshine and plenty."

You will understand why the look of the word "bread" on paper or even the smell of bread baking which sometimes drifts out into a London street, would make me think of Uncle Rufus: when I was fourteen years old Uncle Rufus married a coloured woman who owned a bakery shop. And Uncle Rufus was the most entertaining and mysterious character of my childhood.

While grandfather was alive, Uncle Rufus just lived with the coloured woman, whose name was Coralita Duboisier, in a secret way, though the secret became rather open when they had a family. Still, even the servants were in a conspiracy not to gossip about Uncle Rufus and his family in the hearing of my grandfather; so when we were in bed they would sit on the veranda steps which opened out of the nursery and whisper about him, and we would strain our ears to listen. As they spoke in patois, we took the trouble to learn that fascinating language from the cook's daughter. In this way we got to know the names of all our illegitimate cousins, their bad and good habits, their mother's extraordinary charm in spite of bow-legs and a squint, and the way in which Uncle Rufus would run through grandfather's allowance and then borrow from Coralita's bakery till. As he was the last male in what was fast becoming a matriarchy, Uncle Rufus was invested with a glamour which even his carrot-coloured hair and boorish manners did nothing to dissipate.

We were conscious that being white, and being girls, we would have to grow up properly and correctly, and for these reasons we were bitterly jealous of Coralita, and curious about the assortment of plain and pretty, light and dark babies which she and Uncle Rufus had speedily accumulated. It was queer, but with the exception of the eldest, Virginia, the light children were the plain ones and the dark children were the handsome ones; it was as though nature had tried hard to be impartial, handing out spread noses and large mouths to those with gingery hair and pale skins, and straight high noses and small voluptuous lips to those whose skin was golden-brown and whose hair was more than curly. But Virginia, the first-born, had all the best qualities of both races: her colour was pale golden, her hair copper brown with soft waves, her limbs douce and oriental, and her eyes brown and innocent.

Whenever we passed Coralita's bakery on our way to the botanical gardens we would say to our nurse: "We know whose shop that is, ha, ha," and she would say: "Be quiet, children, do." Such a lovely smell came out of the shop, which had great stone ovens, charcoal fed, at the back, and the palms at the gate leaned back towards the roof and seemed to be bending down to sniff the lovely rich aroma. And our nurse would say: "Remember you're white, and think of your grandfather." But after a while this admonition lost some of its force, for grandfather died.

Then there began a brief struggle between grandmother and the aunts on one side, and Coralita and the priests on the other, for the body of Uncle Rufus. I can only say the body, for in those days Uncle Rufus showed small indication of having a mind. But the priests said that he had a soul, and that he was committing mortal sin. And when Coralita was having her seventh baby they told him that she was in danger of dying, and made him promise to marry her. So after the baby was born it was given grandfather's names at a grand double ceremony, which was both a christening and a wedding, and the other children were all bridesmaids and pages. Our nurse told us that Virginia looked like one of God's little angels in turquoise-blue satin. We wept angrily into our pillows that night because we had not been invited, and because the aunts would not let us go to the cathedral – not even to hide behind a pew and peep. At about that time the aunts had a consultation and decided that we were growing too old to remain in the island, and that we must go to school in England.

There was no one on whom we could depend for news of Uncle Rufus, for our nurse was not much of a correspondent. But gradually items of news about him crept into the aunts' letters, and we gathered that in some strange way Uncle Rufus was getting respectable. Uncle Rufus had espoused the cause of the labourers. Having married a coloured woman, he had thrown in his lot with her people. He was the first white man to shake hands with a visiting trade unionist. He was in the town council. He was a radical. He was getting fatter. He was in the legislative council. He was the mayor. He was nearly as popular as Coralita's bakery.

The aunts even began to mention him in their letters as if they thought we were getting old enough to share a dubious joke with them. "Just fancy, Uncle Rufus has taken Coralita to call at Government House. Virginia is really a very nice-looking girl, considering...They say he lives like a sultan, doesn't even take his own boots off. His children adore him and behave like house-slaves. They say he sleeps with a pistol under his pillow, having announced that he will shoot down any white man who attempts to flirt with Virginia." And then, long afterwards: "You will be surprised to hear that Aunt Julie and I have at last called on Coralita. We found her as ugly close-to as she was at a distance, but very kind and quite modest (strange to say). It was odd being in a house full of children again. I must say that they were very happy children, and quite respectful, for they called us Miss all the time. We had a lovely tea, and of course Coralita was very proud of her fresh-baked bread."

One day, when the guns and bombs first began to roar all over London, I stood looking in at a bakery window and beside me stood a little girl and her mother. The guns began snapping in the suburbs, and the little girl said, with her eyes fixed on a tray of cakes, "Is someone angry, to make such a lot of noise? Is someone cross?" She was listening to the din, gripping her mother's hand and staring at the cakes. It seemed to me that everyone in the world was angry or in danger except the people living so safely and happily in that island, except Uncle Rufus living like a sultan in the midst of his growing sons and daughters.

So now you will understand why I thought of Uncle Rufus when I read the letter. For who could have imagined that the ovens in that island would ever grow cold for want of wheat, or that the smiles would die on the golden and brown faces – that Uncle Rufus could possibly get thin, and that people would be angry and violent everywhere, everywhere in the world, even in the street outside Coralita's bakery.

A TALK ON CHINA

He pressed the bell with the cheerful boldness of an old friend and stood there beaming behind his glasses: a little Catholic chaplain in Allied uniform, wearing under his military cap the ingratiating smile of someone who is about to beg a favour or tell an impossible story. Stella had seen such an expression on the nuns' faces when they called to ask for funds for their orphans.

"But I can't talk to you," she said. "I can't talk to you and I can't give you any money, for I am just about to catch a train. I must – I've got to give a lecture to some schoolgirls. Seven hundred of them, in fact. A talk on China."

"But pardon me." The priest inserted into the half-open doorway one of his bony knees, which were encased in khaki breeches.

"Do not send me away. I come from your homeland, and have only just arrived in England. I bring you a message from your illegitimate cousin Mirabelle. My name is Father Grolier."

Mirabelle: homeland. The two words rang so sweetly in the chill of the corridor that Stella immediately admitted the clerical ambassador, who followed her indoors to an oval table on which her notes lay pale beneath the three dying daffodils. The sad look on the notes and the accusing hands of the clock reminded her that her urgent problem was one of contraction: how to squeeze four thousand years of mellowing Chinese civilisation into twenty-five minutes for the ten to twelves and thirty minutes for the twelve to fourteens. A more craven spirit would have sagged beneath the enormity of the assignment; but Stella was far more disturbed by the presence of Father Grolier and the condition of the flat which she was about to abandon for the day. Now I shall never have time to tear the beds apart and slap all the dishes into the cupboard, she sighed, her eyes lighting gloomily on the words T'ang dynasty, guerrilla factories, progress of women.

"Then Mirabelle..." she slipped one arm into a sleeve of her outdoor coat. Looking straight into Father Grolier's eyes she saw that they were green as green as the palm-festooned island on which there lived a girl with brown laughing eyes. "But I must hurry!"

"Where are you going?" As he spoke Stella saw on his face a gleam of liberation and the love of adventure. She told him the name of the suburb; he had never heard of it, and she had little idea where it was. "Never mind, we shall find it together, and on the way we shall talk, for I have a great deal to tell you," he said. Together they snatched up notes, gloves and a bag and ran for the bus.

"Shall I tell you about myself first?" They were now in front of the tube booking office. "Well, may I explain that I have met also your mother, but only in the distant manner of those who participate in cups of tea but do not share a faith. I was very interested to meet her, for being a country priest I had hitherto met in the confessional only those members of your family whose mixed blood adds so greatly to the charm of East Indian types – I refer of course to the illegitimate children of your uncles, your great-uncles, and your great-grandfather."

He paused for breath and to push Stella firmly into a seat, dislodging with courtesy a fat woman and taking up her position. His voice was foreign and clear and had a pulpit attraction for the midday tube passengers, despite the loud whirring of the train.

"People, people, so many people, as thick as the trees in your lovely island! Back in the presbytery, my old housekeeper was deaf, and I had to seek out my parishioners on horseback through a jungle. Imagine, I had come from a lively town in Europe where every scandal, every venal sin even, was a public concern. I loved the beauties of nature and solitude, but after three years of that jungle I seized with joy the opportunity to join our fighting forces over here, for as you see, I am still young." He stooped to pick up Stella's gloves, which had slipped to the floor.

"Thank you. And please may I have my notes?" She took the papers from him and modestly cast her eyes on the words: T'ang dynasty. Golden age of Poetry. Comparable.

"We have a few Indo-Chinese in my unit," said Father Grolier. "Did I tell you that I am assistant censor? It is quite like a continuation of my work in the confessional. Of course the things which interest me most are the problems of marriage and sex. These things are human. They are universal."

Ah, well, thought Stella, I am not keeping my end up; I am cheating the tube public. She smiled and responded in a voice which was more audible than usual: "Did you ever hear the Chinese proverb, 'If a man is unfaithful to his wife, it is like spitting from a house into the street, but if a woman is unfaithful to her husband, it is like spitting from the street into the house'?"

"Very profound, and confirming my personal observations. Is it not strange how often a white man will live in happiness with a coloured women and how seldom a coloured man will remain faithful to a white woman, even though she is said to be his superior? But there is another matter connected with your homeland, which has puzzled me for a long while. Why, when there is so much rushing water for electric power in the island, did the government install a machine running on oil which has to come from abroad? These matters are great mysteries."

The Chinese Industrial Co-operatives create for refugees a new interest in life. Thousands of crippled soldiers and refugees are employed on these projects, read Stella. "And Mirabelle? Is she a mystery too?"

"Mirabelle is the most European of all your cousins," said Father Grolier. "She longs to come over here and join the ATS. Actually, that is why she asked me to call. She would like you to get an MP to take the matter up in the House of Commons. She does not think it is fair that the boys who volunteer should get free transport to England to join the forces while she has to teach embroidery at the convent. She is very angry about this. But she is beautiful, Mirabelle! And modern! England is full of army captains who are starving for beautiful wives like Mirabelle."

The train groaned into a suburban station. Father Grolier regarded the station clock with pleasure. "We are early. Allow me to take you out to lunch before your lecture. When I take people out to lunch I always patronise the best restaurant, which is generally in the most expensive hotel. Let us go in search of one."

"Oh, no!" cried Stella. "Remember that we have another bus ride – to the school. Besides I always eat at an Express Dairy. I can see one across the street." Disappointed, Father Grolier took her arm and led her to a spotty table. He looked at her hands pensively. "You are married? You do your own housework? You are happy with your husband?"

"I ought to warn you," countered Stella, "that this school at which I am to talk is a progressive one. They will be rather surprised to see me arriving with a priest."

"By progressive," said Father Grolier, "you mean advanced?"

"Well...I mean progressive," said Stella.

"Are you progressive?" he asked.

"Of course, the expression is a little dated, " she said.

"I am not affected by dates," said Father Grolier solemnly. "My calendar is the encyclical of the human soul."

The waitress approached, and he ordered two steak and kidney puddings, adding: "And please being me a bottle of red wine or two beers."

"I'm sorry, sir, we do not serve intoxicating drinks in this establishment," said the waitress.

"Then bring us two large black coffees as soon as possible, please." Father Grolier drummed on the table. He returned to Stella, fixing her with his green eyes. "Are you busy this evening? I should like to invite you to the theatre. How wonderful it is to see life enacted on a stage! In a moment you are in the interior of a home; you see the domestic tragedy, or comedy. Frequently when I watch these happenings I feel a desire to climb on the stage and give the players a little advice."

Now, is he laughing at me or is he really so impossible asked Stella of herself, saying: "I'm very sorry. But I have to cook the dinner tonight."

"You are a devoted wife." Father Grolier's voice was a compound of regret and admiration. "Tell me – for I am always very interested – what is it that keeps you united to your husband? For I have found that there is great need in marriage for a common enthusiasm..."

A distress amounting to indigestion afflicted Stella. She saw China receding into the distance and the mocking palm-girt eyes of Father Grolier coming nearer and nearer. (I shall never get through this lecture. I have forgotten every word of it.) "In our case," she said, swallowing desperately, "I expect it is politics."

Now it was Father Grolier's turn to be distressed. After a pause during which he emptied his coffee-cup, he said: "I am not so sure that it would be a good thing for Mirabelle to take the risk of being interned or of running through the U-boats."

They went out to catch the local bus. It was late; when they arrived at the school a little girl ran panting inside to inform the principal.

The school buildings were stark and new, flung together in haste. Surprised grown-up faces appeared at the windows of the principal's office; in a few moments introductions were effected, and Stella made a strategic effort to get the principal into the staff lavatory so that she could explain Father Grolier. "I've never seen him before," she said weakly. "He just arrived – from my homeland – with a message from –"

"Oh, I expect we can squeeze him in somewhere," said the principal, her face clearing slightly. "You realise, of course, that you will have to give your talk twice. Do you think your friend will wish to listen to both lectures?"

But Father Grolier had already decided for himself. He was in the principal's office discussing co-education with the geography mistress, a handsome girl with black hair and red cheeks. "After the first talk, Miss Newcombe has kindly offered to show me over the school."

The children were sitting on the floor of the large hall, cross-legged and packed tight. Against the western wall Father Grolier sat on a bench between the principal and the geography mistress. For a cold moment Stella felt that she was trespassing in Father Grolier's church, that she had stolen his pulpit. Whose was this calm undisconcerted voice speaking to the English young about Young China? Could it be her own? Was she speaking about China or about her homeland?

The children were listening, their faces a sea of county council flowers. "And so, just imagine a girl only a little bigger than yourselves, to whom the whole of life is an adventure,"

Stella found herself saying. "The Japanese have bombed her school, but she has helped to build it again with her own hands. She feels that she is as good as any boy, and as brave. In a little while she may be in the Chinese army, fighting beside the boys or caring for the wounded. In the olden days she might have sat at home behind the quiet walls of a courtyard doing beautiful embroidery like a girl in a convent. But this is new China, where girls are becoming free and equal at last..."

All the eager faces were Mirabelle's face. They, too, wanted to be as good as any boy anywhere in the world. And though they were more afraid of poetry than of machine-guns, they gulped down a T'ang dynasty poem like little fishes, coming up with shining wide-open mouths for more. But suddenly Stella glanced at Father Grolier. How mocking were those green eyes, which said as clearly as possible that some girls would be happier embroidering dragons than struggling for equality! Stella thought with dismay of the mocking voices of the comrades. "After all, Chiang is only another dictator – almost feudal. Corruption in Chungking...struggles in the Kuomintang...the women in the interior are not even liberated yet..."

These thoughts were deep behind her words, which had been continuing evenly. She looked out of the window. All around the gaunt school buildings were the chimneys of factories. "I expect," she went on, "that most of your fathers and brothers work in nearby factories or are in the services, and that you think factories must be very dull places. But let me tell you about the most exciting factories in the world, the guerrilla factories of China."

Twenty-three minutes. The talk was over. Some of the little girls had cramps because they had not wriggled. A great rattle of limbs and pennies sounded through the hall; the head girls were bringing up to the platform bags full of their collection for the suffering children of Free China. To Father Grolier the clinking sound must have been almost too reminiscent, for he tiptoed out in the wake of the beautiful geography teacher throwing back at Stella a deprecatory smile.

When the pennies had been transmuted into a cheque for relief and the good-byes said, Stella walked slowly down the road towards the bus stop. There was only one passenger waiting, half-leaning against the urban bank of grass and dust behind the pavement. Upon this bank he had laid his military cap. (He seems just like a man and not a priest at all was her thought.) "I waited for you," said Father Grolier simply, "to continue our talk."

Stella was tired; but the peculiar thing was that she was glad to see him. He had come and gone – a temporary disturbing influence – leaving something unfinished. Sitting on the stubbly grass beside him, she said: "But I've talked too much already."

"We've just missed a bus. I expect you think me a nuisance. I talk along certain lines. But yes! I watched your expressions. You see, I feel that I am in a strange country, and can say what I please. It is funny. People must feel like that when they come to me in the confessional. When I listened to your talk, I thought that you were preaching at me." He laughed, but without mockery. "You seemed like a young priest. You made me think of Mirabelle, too."

Some of the children who had been in the great hall drifted past, and stared at them curiously.

"The fact is –" Father Grolier coloured a shy salmon-pink – "the fact is, I feel myself to be suddenly a different person since I am over here, just ordinary. I say to myself, 'Religion? It means different things to various people.' And this is something strange for a priest to admit. When you said progressive in the restaurant, your tone was pious. You laugh! But you were giving those children a sermon about a new life. A sermon, but decidedly a sermon. It was just another way of saying 'love thy neighbour'. I could have done some of it better myself. But the part about freedom...that's something I could not have done, because I doubt if I have ever been free, if anyone is free. I think if I should ask you, 'Do you believe in God?' You would say, 'No. Certainly not your God.' And if you were to ask me, 'Do you believe in freedom?' I would say, 'No. There is no freedom. We are all slaves to our early memories, our training, our families and our vows.' I might have said that, I mean. But listen to my freedom of speech now! I will tell you something, I will make you my confession: I love Mirabelle."

He looked at Stella, expecting her to speak; but as she remained silent, he went on: "I don't know why I speak to you this way: perhaps it is because when you spoke to those children you seemed to be in love with a whole country – with the Chinese people – with the world. When I heard your voice, sounding so much in love with great masses of unknown people, I thought to myself Bon Dieu, she may be in love with the masses, but I am in love with an individual, with Mirabelle!"

The bus was lumbering towards them. They rose and regarded each other gravely. Father Grolier said, very simply, the salmon pink fading from his face, "Yes, I love her as a man loves a woman, and I shall never see her again." They climbed onto the bus, and he paid both fares with his earlier hearty flourish. But although Stella expected him to embarrass the passengers with intimate conversation, he remained silent until the moment came for parting.

MISS GARTHSIDE'S GREENHOUSE

"But what a marvellous collection!" I cried. "I've never seen anything like it! Wherever did you get them all?"

The chief librarian smiled. Was it my fancy, or did he smile somewhat moodily?

"We owe them to Miss Garthside. That is, she owed them to us first; and now we owe them to her. It's an odd story…"

"This gorgeous plate, for instance!" I exclaimed. The volume was enormous, lavishly gilt-edged, and under gossamer tissue a life-size, ruby-breasted hummingbird hung above one of the rarer Cattleya orchids. One whole shelf in the special room was taken up by these magnificent books on the flora and fauna of Venezuela. On that wintry evening the very sight of the pages transported me to a brilliant sizzling continent.

"She was one of our borrowers," said the chief librarian. "I cannot call her a subscriber, for as you know this is a free library. Well, we try to keep up a reputation for service and all that. I'm bound to say Miss Garthside made full use of it." He pursed his lips in melancholy reminiscence.

"Of course she paid her fines – as far as I remember, she never had a book out which was not eventually overdue. She kept things so long, you see. But most of the books she read were large and expensive. You know we try and obtain for readers the books they especially ask for. Miss Garthside was forever requesting some work that was practically unobtainable. Yet the committee was very accommodating. They seemed to enjoy indulging her. She never asked for trash, anyhow."

"And I take it she was singularly charming?" – I rather enjoyed pulling the chief librarian's leg.

But at this he hummed and hawed and looked dubious. "No, I can't say she was. She was a plain old thing, lived quite frugally, and always seemed to wear the same grey tweed costume. Had a certain persuasive manner, of course. But wasn't a femme fatale, or anything like that – "

"Was she a botanist, then?"

"No, that wasn't why these books fascinated her. It was simply homesickness. She came from Venezuela, you see. Always said she couldn't stand the winter without her flora and fauna. We used to call this shelf 'Miss Garthside's Greenhouse'. Birds, too. She had orchids and birds in her bonnet, that poor lady."

I opened another volume. There was a beautiful engraving of a stick insect crawling towards a hibiscus flower. The jutting pistil showered miniature blossoms from a stamen like a painted trumpet.

The chief librarian said: "Nostalgie des tropiques. That's what she used to say. 'Mr Hartley, I've got a bad attack of nostalgie des tropiques.' In her remarkably bad accent. But one day her father died. We were all surprised to hear that Miss Garthside had a father. She seemed so old – ageless, somehow."

"So he left her a fortune – and she repaid you for all the books that the poor ratepayer had provided!"

"Not so fast, my dear boy. No, he didn't leave her a fortune. Just a small sum – a few hundred pounds, I believe. It came one February day, and I recall how excited the dear lady was. 'At last! My winter dream will come true. I can go home. Away from all this greyness – to the bright colours of the warm south!' She'd never been able to get even as far as Cannes, you see. So poor. We were all very happy for her. She insisted on taking the first cargo boat out, after she got her passport. She came here to say goodbye. Dear me, it was most touching. Holding my hand and all that. 'Mr Hartley, these books have kept me alive, kept me going all these years so that I could go home.' Quite like a young girl – 'blissfully happy!' – she kept repeating. We felt upset when we saw that her ship had gone through terrific gales. But she arrived all right – I had an airmail letter. I think I replied to it quite promptly, but it was several months before I heard from her again. And before her letter reached me, she had died."

I was silent. What was there to say? To me, Miss Garthside was just another old eccentric; but it was easy to see that the chief librarian had thought her positively loveable.

"The letter is tucked away somewhere, I believe…But the long and short of it was that Miss Garthside's greenhouse was more agreeable than the real Venezuelan landscape – for her, anyhow. She suffered out there, you see. She had remembered the hummingbirds, but forgotten the mosquitoes and scorpions. She had remembered the kind servants – all of whom had departed – and forgotten the native birds of prey. She had gone from a borough where she got free medical attention to a place where it cost a fortune to be transported to hospital and have an operation. Worst of all, the change of climate and the blinding sunshine affected her eyes. Poor Miss Garthside died in darkness."

"What a sad story!" I said, a little clumsily.

The chief librarian looked shocked. "A sad story? Nothing of the kind my boy – a heroic story. You might as well say that Miss Garthside died to leave these books to the library. She died for her greenhouse, in fact. We discovered afterward through a lawyer that she had sufficient funds to fly to Caracas and have that major operation. She even had a relative there who might have taken her in for the rest of her life. But she was afraid that if she did that, she wouldn't be able to pay for the books, and as she had written to me, 'Those books gave me the happiest evenings of my existence.' You see," said the chief librarian loyally, "for all the dreaming and fancying she did among the leaves and orchids and birds in our old books, Miss Garthside was practical and consistent – in fact, a perfect lady."

THE YELLOW HORSE

I don't usually dream, the young woman told me, but the night before it happened I dreamed that I was standing in a field of wild flowers, and curiously enough they were a mixture of orchids and edelweiss, growing thick and close on the ground. As I moved away in my dream, a herd of cattle stampeded over the field and crushed the flowers to a pulp.

Well, when we opened our eyes the next morning we saw Anne standing between our beds in a little sleeper which was getting ragged with wear. She looked at us critically. Something had flown over her during the night and changed her from a baby girl into a little girl who was growing up very fast. She reminded us immediately that we had promised to take her to the merry-go-round on the first warm day. The merry-go-round, she said, grinning as if she had already got one foot in the stirrups. You promised. The first warm day. I know it's warm because I opened the window and leaned out and my fingernails stayed the same colour.

We didn't really want to take her. She looked too clean and wistful. We told her that merry-go-rounds were germy, her mother had caught chickenpox on one. We told her that the merry-go-round hadn't opened up for the season, and she answered that it certainly had, she heard them tuning it up yesterday. You promised, she said.

Nick had nothing to do that day: he was only working part-time. Anne made us get ready very early, and we wore our best clothes. She led us to the car as if she had invited us out for the first time. Whenever we saw her standing on the running board of our bedraggled sports coupé, we remembered that it had not been bought for a little girl to ride in. Anne had assumed possession very simply. We loved and feared her for the way she had taken out a first mortgage on ourselves and everything that we owned.

We parked the coupé between two trees and Anne hopped out first, flinging herself into the thick of all the other little girls with their spring coats flying open and gay ribbons perched on their heads. But when the crowd disentangled itself into small groups, Anne looked forlorn. She had no group. She came slowly back to us, swinging her short arms and staring at the new grass. We loved her so much then that we wanted to stoop and pick her up and tell her confidently that some day we would buy her a whole park to herself and get lots and lots of little brothers and sisters for her to play with…Anne, dear little Anne, don't be so lonely. Instead we each took a hand and trotted her off to the merry-go-round booth.

We lifted her up so that she could buy her own roll of purple tickets. Six extensive rides for a quarter, ma'am. The merry-go-round man led her around the ringside so that she could choose her own horse. She picked a yellow mount with screaming pink-and-orange reins. The man lifted her up carefully with his black-bitten hands, lifted several other armfuls of squirming anticipation on to other gaudy horses, stepped into the centre of the ring like a magician and started the action to the tune of East Side, West Side. Anne was thrilled and grave. She sat with a stiff back and stared far into the distance. We waved to her, but she was too dignified to wave back.

We became dizzy from watching the horses and were about to wander away when we heard Anne calling to us. She wanted to get down. She wanted the man to stop the show. But Anne, Nick yelled back, the other children haven't had their nickel's worth yet!

"It's Thelma!" Anne shrieked, pink and excited. "I see Thelma out there in a swing. I want to play with Thelma."

We pretended not to hear. The first ride would soon be over. Anne no doubt thought that it would be endless, for tears poured down her cheeks. Nick had an idea. He went over to fetch Thelma. If she'll come, he said dubiously. The last time Thelma had visited us I had to catch the beautiful verminous little gypsy and scrub her. She had not reappeared all winter. She was the only little girl of Anne's age in our neighbourhood, and Anne had pined. Now we determined to make amends, even if we had to say with humility: Thelma, we are sorry that we used Lifebuoy soap on you and combed your hair. Nick had barely reached the swings when the horses stopped tearing around and Anne, with hardly a glance at me, scrambled down and ran toward her friend. I joined them slowly. Thelma would not speak to us. It was her older and dirtier brother who told us that she had been mighty sick with a cold all winter long, since she was over to your house. We thought it wiser to move away into the trees, and very soon Anne and Thelma were jouncing comfortably side by side.

Nick and I stretched out in the grass and talked about the queerness of children, how they could go for weeks without saying a word to each other and for months without seeing each other, and still be boon friends. We felt that Anne was happy, so we did not watch her. Instead we watched a businessman's association running races near the slides. Stupid figures of grey-headed men teetering around on stout legs, wearing the grass down with their large noisy boots. They had been running races ever since we arrived, as if they could not stop, as if they were trying to prove their virility by being juvenile. Nick and I said to each other that it was good to be in a big free country where there were lots of parks for kids to play in, and merry-go-round rides six for a quarter, in spite of these dreadful and pathetic ageing children who would not be found in any other country. Presently we turned our heads and saw that Thelma and Anne had joined hands and were running towards the merry-go-round. We waited until we were reasonably certain that Anne's quarter's worth of rides had come to an end; then we called her.

She was riding the yellow horse again, and Thelma had disappeared. Hey, Anne, we cried. But she affected not to see us. She's doing fine, said the attendant. I figured that if any kid could do that much riding without being sick, she's welcome to a few extra turns.

Anne stayed on the horse until the merry-go-round shut down for the evening. She complained to the man that it was still light. He said he was sorry, but he needed his dinner. She turned to us at last with the mournful look of a prisoner for his gaolers. I don't want to go home. Thelma says she stays here most nights until it gets spooky dark.

Nonsense, said Nick. Thelma went home long ago.

Anne's eyes were full of accusation. Thelma was scared. She was scared you'd wash her in the fountain.

We had no reply; Nick said that he would start the car up, and went off.

Oh, please, said Anne in her smallest and loneliest voice, please let me have a tiny bit more fun…

There weren't many people left in the park. The businessmen were still running around. I looked from them to Anne, who was so really young and eager, and nodded. Anne made the rounds of all the free amusements, calling as she went, just one more swing! Just one more slide! Just one more of everything! In the shadows she spied the longest slide of all. The businessmen were using it as the finish for their races.

She jumped out of her swing and winged her way to it, crying as she ran, just one more slide in the biggest slide!

The men had started: they saw her, but she was too fleet, they were too giddy and ill-controlled to stop. They saw her and probably thought they could avoid her. Most of them did. The rest smashed into her like a stampeding herd, knocked her down and seemed to trample all over her. I had time to think – the cattle! the cattle! the cattle in my dream! – before their boots stopped hoofing the ground, before Anne screamed. I knew that she was alive but I felt that we had lost her. I heard their boots echo while Nick carried her to the car.

To us it was a serious disaster. We could not believe the doctor when he said she was unharmed, except for bad bruises; and yet next morning she had forgotten everything except meeting Thelma. But when we took her to the park again some weeks afterwards, we were anxiously hoping she wouldn't ride the merry-go-round. The yellow horse, she said, was a bad wicked horse. He came alive in the spooky night and bit and kicked children to pieces.

THE NAMING

Somehow or other industrious hands had turned the derelict building into a promising beautiful shell: promising to Paul Kemp because its walls were still bare. He could hang them in his imagination with pictures of quality, push the platform further back and install a Bechstein, fill the hall seats with eager intelligent individuals. Why, he would even hear himself at a poetry reading, pouring out to an appreciative audience his favourite lines –

a dancing shape, an image gay,
to haunt, to startle, and waylay –

Good heavens. He was so bemused with the promise of it all that he gazed around as if he expected to see the dancing shape brush by between Councillor Daglish and the platform. Instead of this aesthetic satisfaction, Paul was uncomfortably aware that he was sitting in a row described (amid giggles) as the married women's trade union: squeezed between his recent acquaintances Mrs Remnant and Mrs Tollington.

The mayor had a long brown face, square-chinned like a French film star's. But his eyes were entirely humourless. Brandishing a piece of paper in his right hand, he gave instructions. "Three names. And don't forget, they must be names of artists, and they must be dead."

A creature not too bright or good, muttered Paul, who was in that desperate condition of wanting to be in love but finding no appropriate object for his rhapsodic longings.

"What kind of artist?" called a voice from the back. "Do singers count?"

"Any kind at all," replied the Mayor. "As long as they're well known, either locally or nationally. And as long as they've passed over."

A little frisson went through Paul; he turned his head uneasily. There was no other attractive person in the hall, and even his own good looks were diminished by the National Health spectacles which long hours in an insurance business and longer hours studying the history of art obliged him to wear. It was an infernal shame that in the hall about to be dedicated to the beauty of art, every staunch art lover was as ugly as sin. Well, not as ugly as sin, for surely sin was striking and daring; these people were simply plain. But it was a pity, just the same.

Mrs Remnant licked her pencil and Mrs Tollington unscrewed her pen. Although he had been waiting for the occasion, it caught Paul quite unprepared. He kept glancing about. He lit a cigarette. He tried to listen to the mayor.

"It is a proud moment for the borough. We all know how much hard work has gone into the making of this arts centre! Not a penny from the government or a blessing from the Arts Council, either. It's all our own. And because it's all our own, let's not pass over local artists in favour of big names. The day of unveiling will be a wonderful day for West Gapping. Several of us thought we'd never live to see the day…"

"Hear, hear," came from Councillor Daglish, in a mellow wheeze.

Mrs Remnant, who had printed Gainsborough in block capitals, drove her pencil forward to inscribe Mabel Bourgeoise; after which she set down Dame Laura Knight. On his other side, Mrs Tollington (slower in starting) jotted down Mabs Bourgeoise in a neat flowing script, adding to this Turner and Constable. Mrs Tollington, openly studying Paul's contribution, whispered reproachfully: "But those are French names." "Well, so is Bourgeoise, for that matter," muttered Paul.

"Quite wrong," said Mrs Remnant. "She lived in the next street to me, Mabs Boojoys did, and she died five years ago."

"Who was she?" Paul dared to ask – but it was too late; the mayor called for silence and the tellers collected the slips. Never mind, he could hear a high-pitched voice singing Rose in the Bud and Because at town hall concerts; he smiled patronisingly. He was too recent an inhabitant to have much influence in the naming of the arts building. But he felt he could rely on the solid good sense of his fellow art lovers. After all, for years these people had hoarded paint and distemper, supplied nails and beaverboard, and given their weekends to the making of the place. He could trust them not to be too incongruous.

The tellers passed bundles up to a pair of scrutineers, who in turn passed their results on to the mayor. His lean unsmiling face deepened its expression of gravity and importance. He cleared his throat.

"It's a very close thing. Almost neck-and-neck. The two leading names are..." he paused, enjoying a suspense which irritated Paul.

"The two leading names are: Joshua Reynolds, twenty-nine votes. Mabel Boojoys, twenty-eight. Constable and Turner tie for third, with seventeen votes each. Watts, seven votes. Landseer five votes. I wish the gentleman who voted for three French impressionists or soorealists or whatever they are would step up here and pronounce the names for me..."

"I told you," said Mrs Tollington, nudging Paul smartly.

"Dame Laura Knight and Alfred Munnings are out, because they aren't dead yet – "

"Nor is Henry Moore," said a voice.

"He only got one vote, anyway. As I was saying, it's neck-and-neck, because I haven't voted yet myself, and after a great deal of consideration..."

"Come on!" growled someone.

"I cannot withstand giving my vote to our grand local artist and much regretted personality Mabel Boojoys."

There were two kinds of moans from the audience: frustrated cries of "out of order!" from Reynolds voters, and agitation from the Boojoys fans. A re-vote was decided upon, and as the tellers passed fresh slips, the mayor remarked judicially:

"Now there may be some of you who voted for the minority

names. Here's your chance. The question before us is, are we going to christen this building with the name of one who (as you might say) gave her life for art in this borough – "

Respectfully low ejaculations came from certain persons.

"Or the name of a great British painter who specialised in portraits of the aristocracy and who is already immortalised?"

"Shame!" grunted Councillor Daglish, but only his close cronies knew what he meant.

A feeling of resignation crept over Paul. He could see that Mrs Remnant had given her vote boldly to the mysterious Mabs Boojoys. Mrs Tollington, looking grim, hid her voting paper under her handbag as she wrote.

"Who was she?" whispered Paul.

"She was my friend," replied Mrs Remnant. "And she painted flowers."

Now the tellers were collected again. It was obvious that the audience was in considerable emotional turmoil; there were a few abstentions.

"Silence, please!" called the mayor, as the scrutineers came forward. "Now for the result." And his face almost lightened into a smile. "I am happy – yes, happy and proud – to announce that Mabel Boojoys has thirty-one votes. Joshua Reynolds got the same as before, twenty-nine. It is therefore my pleasurable duty to declare the choice of name for this new arts centre Boojoys Building. You will all receive invitations to the naming ceremony next month."

Several people looked dejected and disgruntled, but nobody looked as dejected as Paul Kemp. Although he was still accounted a stranger, he had put a lot of his energies and dreams into the completing of the arts building: and he had boasted of it inordinately to his less cultivated friends in other boroughs. It seemed to him dire and fantastic that this house of dreams should be given the disgraceful title of bourgeoise, pronounced Boojoys. Was anyone else aware of the incongruity? He rose trembling, and exclaimed: "But, Mr Mayor, the name of Boojoys, surely..."

"The matter is now settled. Out of order," said the Mayor sharply. With mingled murmurs of disapprobation and congratulation the meeting made its way out into the street.

♦   ♦   ♦   ♦   ♦

Paul was so upset by the whole affair that for a few days he took to catching his bus at an inconvenient stop, so that he would not be forced to pass those walls on which, in livid chromium, the fatally funny letters would shortly be affixed. But a hint of reprieve came to him in the form of a typed notice marked "emergency meeting", hastening him along to the new arts centre on a Wednesday evening. This notice indicated that something urgent had arisen to make necessary a reconsideration of the naming.

Something unkind and unlooked for was in the air and Paul, as if huddling for protection, seated himself again between Mrs Remnant and Mrs Tollington. Two seats away sat the mayor; this time the chair was taken by Councillor Daglish, who rasped and stuttered that the mayor felt he could not preside, owing to personal considerations. "Well, friends," spluttered his malicious old lips, "I know there's been a good deal of talk about the naming of this building. Talk is all very well, and we have to stand by majority decisions, as you know. But when the mayor got some anonymous letters…"

"Shame!" called a man's voice – young and indignant, this time. Paul covered up his nervous anticipation by dragging out a notebook and scribbling in it *a dancing shape, an image gay*. (Dash it, I've got that on the brain, he thought.)

"Letters stating that Mabel Boojoys was unworthy of giving her name to this arts centre – "

"Come, come," said the mayor from the floor, taking advantage of his private capacity. "We decided not to go into the reasons."

"Indeed, and I should think we'd all like to know the reasons!" cried Mrs Remnant aggressively.

"Better not ask," a quiet male speaker intervened.

"There's no one going to cast anonymous aspersions on Mabs Boojoys in my presence, nor in public either," said Mrs Tollington.

Councillor Daglish asked for a vote on the matter. Would the assembly like to hear the reasons? It might be better if the whole thing was hushed up (he frowned at Paul) for the sake of newcomers and outsiders. During the show of hands on this point, Paul, out of loyalty to Mrs Remnant and her group, raised his arm quickly. If he had been appalled before, he was dismayed now; his feeling for the arts centre was sinking lower and lower. It sank to its lowest ebb when he heard Councillor Daglish mumble that Mrs Boojoys had once been guilty of public dishonesty. She had presided over an art show of her own paintings at the town hall, some ten years back, and had pocketed a third of the entrance takings – the stewards had checked.

"Good heavens!" said Paul, but he was only heard by Mrs Remnant, who had a handkerchief to her eyes. "Fancy dragging that up against the poor woman!" Mrs Remnant gulped.

"And that's not all!" cried a shrill feminine voice from the mayor's right. "Remember the painters she had living with her!" Was it the mayoress? At any rate the exclamation came from a little face made of dough, with lashless sockets and a round mouth-hole. Never had Paul so longed for some exquisite creature to slip her arm through his and lead him away.

"She was an artist!" Mrs Tollington almost howled.

"Artists have to be decent same as the rest of us, we can't name our new centre after a woman that wasn't respectable," retorted the shrill voice. Paul then realised that in the show of hands most of the younger women in the room had been in favour of hushing the matter up.

"Well, it's petty and mean…" he began.

"Order!" coughed out Councillor Daglish. "The question now before us is, are we going to vote again on the naming of this centre, or will the house accept the second name on the list, that of J. Reynolds, as the best alternative in this unfortunate situation?"

"I move we accept the name of Reynolds," said someone mildly.

"Doesn't bother me," said a hearty voice. "I'll just consider the place named after my Sunday paper, and so will a lot of people."

The vote was taken, and the dispirited enfeeblement of Mabs Boojoys' partisans resulted in a sweeping majority for Sir Joshua, despite the valiant interjection, "Well, he probably done a lot worse in his time." Alone among the women, Mrs Remnant and Mrs Tollington threw their well-used hands into the smoky air. Paul, ashamed but relieved, sat with his fists on his knee.

◆   ◆   ◆   ◆   ◆

When the funereal gathering dispersed, he could see ahead of him in the street the figures of Mrs Tollington and Mrs Remnant, one on each side of the pavement. They walked with lowered heads, Mrs Tollington – who was a nimble little body – fairly racing along; but Mrs Remnant, who had more weight to carry, was easy to overtake.

"I say – Mrs Remnant – excuse me."

Paul felt it necessary to explain that he was really on the side of Mabs Boojoys, by and large; it was only her name which he had considered from the very first quite unsuitable for an arts centre.

"Her name…," said Mrs Remnant bleakly. "There's certainly not much left of that now." And she lumbered on coldly.

"She must have been an exceptional person, to have such loyal friends as yourself and Mrs Tollington…and the mayor," panted Paul, suddenly succumbing to a curiosity which had mounted within him since the first meeting, to find out what kind of person Mabel Boojoys really was – and above all, what sort of artist she was.

"She was that," said Mrs Remnant.

"I'd like to see some of her work. It may be – well, one never knows. She may have been a great…anyway, perhaps a good artist. Supposing one day some of her paintings hang in the new centre and all those mean little gossips are forced to eat their words?"

"None of her paintings will ever hang in that place," said Mrs Remnant, without slowing down.

"And why not?"

"Because I've got them all – except the ones she sold to the maternity home. Oh dear, my poor head does ache. I do need a cup of tea!"

"And so do I, please, Mrs Remnant," insinuated Paul appealingly. She gave him a nod, which was not inviting, but he followed her into the house and waited while she put the kettle on.

The reviving effect of three cups of strong tea on Mrs Remnant's temperament gained for Paul his objective. She took him up into her attic and dusted off various canvases wrapped in brown paper. The attic was fairly well lit – light enough, at any rate, to display the total mediocrity of Mabel Boojoys' flower paintings.

"Very nice," said Paul. And that was what they were, alas: very nice. Paul felt extremely sad. He longed, for the sake of Mrs Remnant as much as for the vindication of Mabel Boojoys, to have been able to rave in that stuffy attic about the discovery of true unappreciated genius. Douanier Boojoys... But these little masses of well-arranged blossoms evoked nothing from him but wonder at the tremendous industry of the painter – there were so many of them.

"It's just as I told you – she was my friend, and she painted flowers," said Mrs Remnant, beginning to wrap the pathetic squares up again.

"Didn't she paint any portraits?" Paul spoke to cover up his disappointment.

"Only one, and that gives me the creeps. I never did approve of anyone sitting for hours and hours in front of the looking-glass," said Mrs Remnant uninvitingly. "It's that one, over there." She let Paul undo it himself, watching him in superstitious gloom.

At last a mystery was laid bare: the reason for the strong waves of emotion in the meeting-hall proclaimed itself with a dropping of dusty paper. That exquisite narcissistic self-portrait which was the only beautiful thing Mabel Boojoys had painted glimmered like a presence under attic beams. Its bold yet fragile features wore a suffused look of glorious mockery. The portrait was beautiful, not because Mabs Boojoys was an artist (save perhaps in living) but because she was beautiful in herself. During those long hours of concentrated truthfulness before her mirror, she had set it all down.

"Her to the life," said Mrs Remnant.

"Oh, but if only she had gone on living!" cried Paul, recollecting all the plain hefty faces in the arts centre, and how he had gazed around searchingly...for what? For the image gay, the phantom of delight. For this very face, still the most beautiful face in the borough: the face which had dazzled the mayor and come near to making the new arts centre a national laughing stock.

A REAL PERSON

Torch and cigarette, like a big brother and a little brother, moved evenly down the drive between the royal palms: Walter stood on the top veranda and watched his brother Stephen disappear into a car and switch on the larger brilliance of head-lamps. An engine hum broke the silence that had fallen when the washerwoman's birds ceased their squeegee courting noises at sundown. Stephen drove away to his club. He drove through a belt of grapefruit trees that lay between the white house and the mysteries of tropical pleasure and poverty.

Walter, who was considered too young at sixteen for club life, went into his brother's room and filched a packet of cigarettes. He lit one, cleared his throat imposingly, and said aloud, "At last."

Drooping above smoke on the veranda, he saw the cook stroll off down the driveway with a basket on her head. The evening was violet tinged with chartreuse. Walter threw his cigarette on the gravel below and muttered, glancing at the overhanging mountains, "A real person. Get together with a real person."

Before he finished the sentence he lifted the trapdoor to the stairs and lowered himself into the black square, pulling the heavy lid shut after him. He heard a clink of china from the pantry: the maid was setting out a cold supper. A delicate smell of citrus oil stole up from the valley below. Walter sat down on a canvas chair by a square table. A moment later the night watchman dropped into a chair beside him.

"Howdy, Mr Walter."

"Hi," said Walter casually.

The night watchman took out of his ragged pocket a small box and a Bible. He replaced the Bible and spilt on the table a stack of dominoes.

Dominoes was a wicked gambling game in the colony, and the watchman turned them over furtively.

"Stake ten cents," said Walter, laying down a West Indian dime, Queen's head uppermost.

The night watchman grunted.

"Any news?" asked Walter, counting out his tablets and drawing one towards him.

"No murders this week," said the watchman.

"You have the double-six, Ishmael," said Walter.

"A rock like a meteor blasted by the almighty split a woman's house in two and bounced over head while she slep'," said Ishmael. "This country surely is a land of rocks and stones and calamity."

"Ha, ha," said Walter, playing a tablet. Meanwhile the watchman's two familiars crept up and nuzzled the players in turn. One was a cat in evening dress, large and magnificent, with a scarred nose. The other was a small, drab tabby, wife to the larger animal. The tomcat's white shirtfront shone in the starlight.

"Why don't you have a dog?" asked Walter.

"What, for scaring?" asked Ishmael. "These do work better. I'm informing you, the whole town's scared of old Gaga. And Catwife, she sniffs out a thief at a hundred yards, shows it in her whisks. Gaga's the ghost of Mr Bumpton, anyway. Everyone knows that. Not a malefactor in the land would come anywhere near them. All the stealing round here takes place in the daytime, I'm pleased to say."

The maid's voice called from the pantry window, "Mr Walter, supper's laid cold any time."

"Thanks," Walter called back. He followed her steps with alert ears until she finally plonked down with a screech of bedsprings in some concealed vault. He lost two cents to Ishmael, who put down his last ebony rectangle and got up saying, "Well, Mr Walter, I'll do the rounds once. And you please do the usual."

Standing up, Ishmael was visible now by the light from the study window, which made a big triangle on their card-table. He was a brown gnome, aged about thirty-five; not quite a hunchback. He wore a loose, khaki shirt hanging outside a dirtier pair of trousers of the same material. On his head he had a rancher's hat. In his hand he carried a club studded with wicked-looking nails. The two cats moved off with him, but

Catwife came back and lay down beside Walter's sandalled feet.

When Ishmael and Gaga had gone out of sight, Walter got up soundlessly and made for the dining room. He poured out two snifters of rum, turning the bottle so that the label hid the tidemark. He slid back quickly over the polished floor to the table. Catwife was waiting for him, but she had turned towards the dark garden, her rust-coloured nose dilated. Above the insect noises rose the sound of the river, a low river, a river at rest between new and full moon.

"Catwife, you're a darn plain female for old Gaga to associate with," said Walter in a wordy tone, nudging her with his sandal. She ignored him and, rising on her haunches, stiffened her whiskers. Walter looked into the garden. Where the wall was broken he thought he saw something wrapped in a sheet, something black and white like a stage ghost.

"Hi!" he called, and the apparition vanished.

"And whose spirit are you?" he asked Catwife, resisting like any clubman the longing to drink alone. Catwife got up and streaked into the bushes.

After a long pause, Walter began to wonder if Ishmael had stopped to eat dinner on his round. Sometimes he came back to the game with greasy fingers, for he ate with his fingers out of a tin pail like a primitive. Twice he had been sacked for going to sleep with a woman after a heavy meal. Two outhouses had caught fire on the second occasion. But Stephen always rehired him.

"Now why should Mr Bumpton's ghost inhabit Gaga when the fellow died in Trinidad?" asked Walter of himself. As if to reply in person, Gaga loped easily up the stone steps. He gave Walter a malevolent frown, then lay beside him.

At that moment Ishmael and Catwife came along slowly. "Not a malefactor abroad," said Ishmael in his best Biblical manner. He finished chewing. "Met a friend."

"I saw him," said Walter. "Who was he?"

"He was the Buddhist!" Walter lifted his little glass and took a gulp, to conceal emotion. The real person! The person he wanted to meet.

"Takes two baths a week in our river, lacking his own tub," said Ishmael proudly, laying a double-four.

Walter moved a domino dreamily. "Why don't you bring him here? Doesn't he play?"

"He plays, but not for money. And he only drinks milk. Wouldn't suit Mr Stephen," said Ishmael. "Too much of a different man. Thinks too much. Mr Stephen wouldn't like it. Whyn't you get yourself a girl? Or I'll get one for you?"

"I don't want a girl," said Walter. It was untrue: he wanted one badly. But not the kind the night watchman could obtain.

"Your turn," he said sharply.

◆　　◆　　◆　　◆　　◆

"Your turn," said Walter. But this time he was speaking to the Buddhist, and it was full moon. The white eyes of the dominoes and the white eyeballs of the Buddhist flashed sympathetically.

Ishmael had downed his rum in one lick and looked sleepy. Getting a glass of milk for the Buddhist was a harder task than raiding the rum bottle – milk was so much scarcer. Walter had coaxed half a glass from the maid for the cats and, as if aware of this deceit, Gaga and Catwife had curled themselves round the table legs, glaring reproachfully, now and then emitting short, malignant mews like barks.

The Buddhist was a black man, entirely negro, far blacker than Ishmael. His face was long, gentle, and humorous. This had shocked Walter at first, since he had expected a part-oriental at least. He was dressed in an ordinary, fawn linen suit, and what Walter had taken for a ghostly sheet proved to be a large bath towel, which now hung over the veranda rails. If the Buddhist was a thinker, he was chary of thinking aloud. His thoughts had to be drawn from him by questions.

"I see they haven't killed you yet?" Ishmael said pleasantly.

"No," replied the Buddhist. "Not as yet."

"Tee ha ha!" Ishmael laughed. "They hired me to drop a big rock on his head when he was swimming. Man, what a joke of a calamity that was! Budd and me go up cliff together and drop the rock into our river. Kerr-smash-plunk! Just to learn them. Next morning there's a big hole in the cliff, that's evidence. I claim half the cash, saying I miss. Budd and me share it."

"Who paid it?" asked Walter, moving a three-one.

"Plenty people. Plenty good Christians," said Ishmael, "don't fancy him being against religion."

"I am not against religion. I'm not against anybody," said the Buddhist in his courteous drawl.

"Have you any disciples?" Walter asked.

"Only one."

"A goat-keeper," enlarged Ishmael.

"Elsewhere, there are more than a million of us," said the Buddhist.

"Then why do you have to be so different here?" asked Walter in a tone of enthusiastic curiosity. He knew that he was different too, and pleaded for support, for a clue. But he got none. The Buddhist played his last, losing domino, drank the milk and got up.

"I thank you for the entertainment and the good milk."

"Nothing. Come again," said Walter.

"And for your friendship, my brothers," added the Buddhist. "I hope one day" – he looked at Walter – "to be able to give you something."

There were a few drops of milk left in the glass and, tearing a large leaf from the green almond tree by the steps, he shook the drops on it. Both cats sprang up and bent their heads simultaneously. Gaga allowed Catwife to lick the leaf longest, and the Buddhist smiled down at them as if the sight pleased him.

He walked away under the blazing moon towards the faint clank of goat-chains that betrayed where his disciple was crouching in the bushes.

Walter called after him softly, so as not to disturb the maid, "Don't forget. Club night. A week from today."

"I'll certainly come," called back the Buddhist, even more softly.

Before the next club night, Walter got hold of an article on Buddhism and started reading it: "The final goal of the religious man is to escape from existence into blissful non-existence. Individual man is made up of elements that existed before him. They separate at his death and they may be recombined in a somewhat similar fashion."

For all his efforts at concentration, Walter could not help thinking of Mr Bumpton and Gaga.

"The Enlightened One:

1. Existence is suffering.

2. The origin of suffering is desire.

3. Suffering ceases when desire ceases.

4. The way to reach the end of desire is by following the noble eight-fold path."

But Walter could not pursue the noble eight-fold path. The awful thing was that he felt existence to be more blissful than non-existence, and he actually longed to suffer with desire so that he would be full grown at last, a man.

It seemed to him, too, that the Buddhist had put himself beyond temptation, living the way he did on milk and strips of coconut and yams, with only one disciple – and that one a poor, ugly goat-girl clad in rags as dirty as the goats she tended.

Ishmael had only to mention the goat-girl and he would exclaim, "Phfui!" sniffing obscenely.

The goat-girl kept her distance, however, clanking mournfully in the crotons on club nights – perhaps as antipathetic to Ishmael as he was to her, perhaps disapproving of the gambling, for Ishmael and Walter continued to play for money while the Buddhist played for entertainment.

So the club nights went on, exciting in their prospect of an enlightenment which never quite arrived. The moon diminished once more, and Walter was halfway through his school holidays.

◆　　◆　　◆　　◆　　◆

The way in which he learnt of the Buddhist's escape from suffering was simple. Ishmael moved his five-four, looked out at the night, and brushed a firefly from his hat, remarking, "Only a little stone, real small, and the fellow used a sling-shot, but it got Budd in the temple. Bam! He dropped like a zabricot fruit."

"What? Did they kill the Buddhist?" Walter cried in a tone of unaffected anguish.

"And what was he always seeking but to drop dead like that?" asked Ishmael. "Looked for it every day of his life. The way the goat-girl carried on, you'd ha' thought she was a Christian, you'd ha' thought he had a wish to live. Howling that way, I felt ashame' of her."

"I could howl, too," said Walter. His eyes stung.

"You're eight cents down, Mr Walter," said Ishmael. "Well, Budd and me was friends. I done nearly all I could to keep him going but he surely courted that stone. Don't say otherwise."

He picked up his eight cents with a certain diffidence, and added in a tone of self-reproach, "It was yesterday night, and I slep' at the time."

Neither of them had the stomach for another round. Ishmael pushed off suddenly, bending forward with the weight of his failure.

Walter sat on, and the milk he had stolen for the Buddhist shone on the starry darkness. The air was full of the sound of crack-crack beetles, some as large as mice, clenched to high twigs and scraping away like deal fiddlers.

An unbearable feeling of bereavement stole upon Walter. The real person, the enlightened one, was gone. Maybe he had escaped from existence into blissful non-existence, but maybe he had gone somewhere else. The origin of suffering might be desire, but the Buddhist had never acted as if he desired anything. He had seemed a happy man.

◆　　◆　　◆　　◆　　◆

In his unusual and bereft state, Walter looked around for Gaga and Catwife, but they had gone the rounds with Ishmael. He would have given them the milk, talked to them, anything to break the horror of knowing that his new-found friend had left him forever, perhaps to be broken up and reconstituted, as the Buddhist evidently believed, in some other human form. So tense were Walter's thoughts that when he saw something white drifting over the lawn, he cried out.

A voice almost as frightened as his own called back in what seemed like a little sob, "Hush! It's only me, the disciple."

The goat-girl drew near in spurting steps. Amazed to see her, nearly unrecognisable in white and without goats, Walter's welcome was a loud sigh. She came to the lower veranda steps, sat down, and rested her head in her brown hands. The wonderful thing was that she gave out a jasmine scent like the flowers overhead. A silence fell as an interval of relief.

Walter had lost the enlightened one, but someone had come, perhaps another real person, though only a girl. The goat-girl parted her lips to speak, showing teeth as clean as silk-cotton pods, and Walter felt emboldened to study her more closely.

He did not know it, but negro and Carib traits blended in her gentle face. Under a white mourning headcloth, black silk hair fell in springy curls. She pleased Walter intensely.

"The Brother wished to make you a gift, but he left nothing. Only the goats, and you did not love them."

"That is true," he said shyly. He held out the glass of milk. "Please take this."

The goat-girl took the milk and sipped it as if the Buddhist had taught her how to drink it, disregarding thirst and greed.

"He left me nothing, too. So I come to you."

She stared at him with her slanting eyes, and Walter, longing to make the appropriate adult gesture of acceptance but bitterly conscious of how young he was, stammered, "I'm only here during my holidays, you know."

"I do know. That's why I come so soon. I will come again if you want, until you go away."

"I'll be glad of your company."

They ventured melancholy smiles at each other. After a moment Walter sat on the step beside the girl and let his hand rest on hers until the headlamps of Stephen's car blazed down the drive.

The girl at once ran phantom-like over the grass through the palisade of bushes.

He believed she would come back as she had promised, just as he knew that he was suffering for the first time, really suffering, and that only part of the pain was caused by the loss of a friend and by doubt that the enlightened one would have sanctioned the gift. Walter might never resolve the doubt, but at least he was certain that he was blissfully alive, that he was capable of practically anything, and that in spite of the mysterious and inexplicable conflict of faiths and races in the world, it was still a world in which miracles happened.

Snatching up the two cats as they twisted their way between his long legs, he banged their furry cheeks together on a rough embrace and burst into the dining room to meet his brother.

A TIME FOR LOVING

On that December day when the new governor landed, Willie the Clerk came tap-tapping at Mrs Gamotte's chapel window, grimacing to hasten her off her knees and away down to the jetty. You would have thought he was an ally, eager to promote her heart's desire. Yet she distinctly heard him say to the burly white figure in cockaded helmet, after she had pushed her way through crowds to a grass-hummock platform: "Look out Sir – Your Excellency – she's edgin' right up alongside – the lady that wants the marrying licence!" Such treachery stabbed her, but did not deflect her; she pressed on towards the governor, parting her old adversaries, the bank manager and Father Toussaint.

"All I want for Christmas is a licence to perform marriages in my new chapel..." Mrs Gamotte was wearing a noticeable pink blouse, exactly the same colour as her chapel; earrings as bright as its gilt spire bobbed beside her determined brown jaw under the palm-straw hat decorated with large purple and orange flowers. There were so many distractions: with a tearing clank the anchor of the frigate which had dropped the governor into a rowboat slithered upwards, and the frigate whipped out to sea again to quell a riot two islands away. The Mighty Bonito, a retired fisherman, stood humming and grinning next to the harbourmaster. Meanwhile, there was the poor new governor trying to make a speech.

"The hard heart of officialdom…" muttered Mrs Gamotte. But she was not entirely discouraged. Her hope of obtaining a marrying licence always revived during a sentimental season or a big ceremonial occasion. Silenced now by the bank manager, she watched with restrained intolerance the governor's kind lips emitting those cold and crisp accents of the north. She watched, but she did not listen, until a few words drifted against her earrings and darted like hummingbirds into her brain.

"…This flowering land," said the governor. "…Dragging out the imitation holly…ruining your fine digestions by boiling up plum-puddings in the English manner…But I have never encouraged the infliction of petit bourgeois customs on the simple and unspoiled…I should like to think of Christmas in this island as something simple: a time for love. That is all it really is, anyhow…"

"Praise be to God!" cried Mrs Gamotte aloud, with her eyes shut. She saw those blue eyes under their sandy eyelashes (as soon as she blinked hers open) rest on the glowing pink of her blouse and wander swiftly upwards past her earrings to the hat, then to the azure horizon, where the frigate's water-trail crossed the wake of an incoming cargo boat. But the governor hardly paused. He was well away now, elaborating on his favourite theme of the different kinds of love – love of God (here he inclined his head politely towards Father Toussaint); love of lovers (the crowd smiled and swayed); and love of one's fellow men, "upon which," he carried on, "I humbly claim to have lavished my adult life: and doubtless the Colonial Office would underwrite my claim."

At the word "love" the Mighty Bonito, now a champion calypsonian, shuddering beneath a passion of creativeness, switched to the tune of a new song he had just that instant created:

> *Oh Christmas is a time for loving*
> *– For loving the Gov-er-nor!*

Mrs Gamotte had edged up to Willie the Clerk now, and she plucked at his free arm. With the other he was stiffly holding a large cream sunshade lined with green over his excellency's head. "What for did you pull me off – of my prayers today only to obstruct me?" she complained. But Willie, who was very tall, craned his head over hers and winked at the harbourmaster, who broke away and dashed downhill, signalling to various customs officials. Boatmen pushed off from the spindly jetty, and the speechmaking ended as it had begun, with cries of acclamation, Mrs Gamotte's murmurings, Mighty Bonito's humming, and the loud metallic rattle of an anchor. The cargo boat had arrived in the bay.

Disappointed and bemused, Mrs Gamotte found herself walking home beside the bank manager. As they rounded the curve of the bay and came to that hidden bite in the shore where her chapel spiked away to the seascape from the bank manager's bedroom window, they saw that a grey schooner had flapped to rest alongside. Its creaking deck swarmed with passengers. Surely these were no neighbouring islanders or even tourists? The newcomers were like Phoenicians out of a poem, landing secretly…although in the full glitter of the sun.

"I shall telephone the harbourmaster at once," said the bank manager; as he went into his house the invaders started dragging from the schooner's deck gaudy shafts, wheels and bright furled canvas hoods, which they began to lower into the water. Several barefoot and barely clothed local youths who had gathered on the beach plunged into the sea and swam or rowed out to the schooner. These spontaneous helpers towed the dismantled caravans on rafts and old canoes, at last bringing their dangerously overloaded freight safe ashore. Gypsies crowded into the last two row-boats, waving thanks to the captain and his crew of three, who stood languid on deck in dirty white duck uniforms, speaking French.

Shaken from her daze of melancholy abstraction, Mrs Gamotte bustled forward to welcome the strangers. She enticed them into the chapel and, seating them in rows of pews, served them glasses of orange-juice; for in her curtained vestry she kept various objects such as a fly-proof larder, a trestle-bed, a crucifix, a bust of Queen Nefertiti, and a sewing basket.

One of the many excuses why her marrying licence had not been granted was that she hadn't any youthful marriageable parishioners, so Mrs Gamotte was disappointed to see only one young creature among the lot. A beautiful girl, half-dead with heat and fatigue, leaned against a vulture of an old crone. Beside her companion's veined ankles and cracked toenails, her delicate sandalled feet were like a reproach.

Swiftly the gypsies drained their orange drinks and went back to the beach, assembling and dragging the caravans on to the road. They thanked Mrs Gamotte in English, but spoke among themselves a sort of slang Latin. Excluded, she straightened her straw hat and marched off to government office. But there she was also excluded: the office was full of gypsies – other gypsies who had come to ask permission to pitch tents on the public savannah. These people had just landed from the cargo boat, and when later they were asked by Willie the Clerk whether they were connected with the travellers by schooner, they said they had nothing to do with them. They said it roughly: "We have nothing to do with them!"

The islanders didn't believe this. They were certain that all these gypsies were friends and relations, like the "Syrians", landing to relieve them of cash in return for Christmas goods. But soon gossip leaked through about troubles back in the Balkan states and all over Europe, about a long feud and a never-ending chase, as if those enemy tribes could not bear either to mingle or to leave each other alone. Blood had been shed between them, it was rumoured.

Father Toussaint put plenty of warnings into his sermons about ignoring pagan prophecies, but when the foreigners began their fortune telling, his congregations were sorely tempted, and sneaked towards the tents and caravans through each short purple dusk. The tribe in the tent told the best fortunes. They had a family of young children – little vagabond dukes leading up to the eldest brother, a handsome Egyptian-looking princeling.

Mrs Gamotte had her future predicted on Monday, Wednesday and Friday by the old crone grandmother of the caravans: and on Tuesday, Thursday and Sunday by various middle-aged women in the tents. They all told her that her wish would come true. She did not indulge in this heart's balm on Saturday, since, like other longer-established religions, she observed the Sabbath on that day. One Thursday evening she saw the Egyptian for the first time.

The sight of him gave her a pang of delight as keen as early passion, so that she nearly missed noticing the governor on a chestnut mare riding off for an exploration of the interior, with Willie trotting behind him on a mule: those were the days when modes of transport indicated social status. The next day she spent many hours on her knees, then she walked up and down the aisle, then she sewed in her vestry upon a splendid length of silver satin intended for an altar cloth.

Soon she found excuses for running between the gypsy tribes like a hungry mongoose. Alone of all the island's gossips, she had learned the names of the beautiful young people in the rival encampments: Janosek and Signata. She pursued her mysterious purpose, whispered those names in the starlight, one against tangled tumbling hair, another into a pallid arrogant ear. It fell to Willie the Clerk to tell her of the great outcry of rage, which arose from the gypsy camps when Janosek and Signata eloped into the wild hills.

The young gypsies' elopement was a peak in the series of unlawful acts which Father Toussaint and the bank manager attributed to new leadership. All that talk about a time for loving! Never had there been such an orgy of lovemaking, singing and feasting in the island! Mighty Bonito's songs were getting more and more obscene. And stealing, too – that was because of the things the new governor had said about poverty and sharing. It was a scandal, when what the island needed was a firm hand and moral guidance. Christmas Eve was drawing near, and the people had already begun to celebrate: not by church going, but by drum beating and rum-swilling. The bank manager's only consolation was that with all the commotion brought on by the gypsies, there was always an endless chain of persons waiting to complain to the governor; and Mrs Gamotte's petition was thus effectively held off. But Mrs Gamotte did not even seem frustrated; rather she behaved like a waiting priestess.

One night the lanky form of Willie appeared in her chapel doorway, to inform her how hunger had defeated the gypsy lovers, as it defeats most fugitives. After living on yams and fruit for three days, the young couple had emerged from the rain forest. They had been captured by island police and marshalled down rocky paths towards the town. It was then dark, and for their protection the governor had given orders that they should be held in the prison.

Mrs Gamotte fell on her knees, loudly praying for the governor to be forgiven the harshness of such an act. The governor who had said it was a time for loving!

Willie smiled slyly: "But the gaol is full of pig and chicken thieves and petty larceny men. Only one cell was empty: the big one with jasmine over the bars where they put white and light coloured people. We put them both into that!" Willie described how the lovers were earth-stained, scratched by prickles, and tired to death, but neither frightened nor unhappy. They had put up no resistance to the police, simply asking to be protected from their families. "We done no wrong," Janosek told the keeper proudly. "Only we love, see? We love."

"Tell that to the governor," hooted the fat keeper.

Just the same, said Willie, Keeper was a decent fellow, and gave them a coco-paille to lie on; he put a piece of mosquito netting over the bars against mosquitoes and peepers, and provided them with water, fish and bread. "And if you like," Willie wound up grandly, "you can go with me to see them in the morning; I have a letter to carry."

Early next morning Mrs Gamotte, bearing a brown-paper parcel, went to the prison with Willie the Clerk. The warring gypsy tribes would not long remain in ignorance of the capture; the prison had come to life suddenly. Wonderful strains of song in a strange Latiny tongue could be heard from behind those grey walls; and Mighty Bonito, standing on an upturned lime-vat near the gates, was leading the prisoners' chorus in his new calypso refrain:

> *De day dat de gov-er-nor came and de gypsies came*
> *Bonito-Boy made a song for to bring dem fame*
> *Because it was near de time of de Christmas dinner…*
> ("De Christmas dinner!" chanted the prisoners sadly.)

It was de time for loving de saint and sinner.
Oh Christmas is a time for loving,
For loving de gov-er-nor.

The song pulsated with human kindness, and was singularly devoid of Mighty Bonito's malicious allusions. The verses numbered eight. The junior warder was beating time on his desk; with every appearance of ushering along distinguished visitors, he broke off and led Mrs Gamotte and Willie to the gypsies' cell.

Signata and Janosek reclined on their coconut mattress, their heads against the stony western wall of the cell; her cheek was against his shoulder and their hands were clasped. Soap had evidently been supplied, for their faces were clean and shining, and their eyes were shining too.

Janosek rose and made room for Mrs Gamotte on the palliasse, seizing her hands warmly. The young people were as pleased as householders entertaining a special visitor.

From the doctor's garden next door came the sound of birds singing and children playing; from the street the song of Mighty Bonito and the deep melancholy chorus creeping out of the prison crevices. Silent and lovely, her lips rose-warm, the gypsy girl gave susceptible Willie a half-smile, then turned the full light of her Romany eyes on Janosek, in trust and delight. Janosek said jauntily: "We like it here. We will not leave. It's a nice prison." He pressed Signata's hand, and she sighed too: "We like it."

They liked everything. They were so happy that all they could say was: "We like. We love."

Panting to describe the scene to the governor, Willie dashed out, leaving Mrs Gamotte in the cell. Gazing upon the lovers in friendly cunning, she unwrapped her parcel, talking soothingly.

That afternoon the governor held an informal council. He consulted four citizens who might help him avert the tragedy hanging over the gypsy lovers, for a pitched battle was brewing upon the savannah. At early moonrise of the following evening...Christmas Eve...the truant couple were whisked inside the police van, then transferred to the bank manager's car and driven briskly down to Mrs Gamotte's chapel.

There in the aisle stood the governor, debonair and rash, a red rose in his buttonhole. The gypsy bride wore Mrs Gamotte's silver cloth like a sari. Willie was the best man. The bank manager and the harbourmaster were witnesses. Looking like a dark female Don in her alpaca robes, Mrs Gamotte revealed with pride her sonorous plain-chant voice and new register book. Everything was as irregular as the most romantic person could have wished; the hour was nearly midnight, the tropical moon was blazing silver. The bride's ring was silver, too, and the bridegroom's only property was a few pound notes which the bank manager and the governor had subscribed. Touchingly elegant and confident the lovers were, clinging to each other under the slithering palms on their way to the rowboat, blessed by their friends as the oars dipped and sparkled. "You'd better get married again properly in Martinique!" called out the bank manager; but they did not seem to hear.

The four on the sand lingered to watch the filling sails and hear the rusty screeching of hawsers, but they did not wait to see the ghostly schooner dim and disappear.

"In a few years she'll be a slatternly old shrew burdened with too many children," said the bank manager severely to Mrs Gamotte.

"Oh, no – not for me, anyhow," intervened the governor. "I shall invariably think of them as eternally young and beautiful, constant and enchanted, and perpetually in love."

Bells were pealing in the town. They sounded like wedding bells, but the harbourmaster exclaimed: "Good heavens, I promised Father Toussaint to be at midnight mass!" He cranked up the bank manager's car, and the two good Catholics drove off.

Willie untied his mule and the governor's mare from the flamboyant tree near the chapel. Mrs Gamotte stood looking out to sea, a salt wind flapping her collegiate gown, but she turned politely as the governor mounted.

"A happy Christmas!" called out the governor, heading his mare towards the savannah.

"Praise be to God and thanks to your Excellency!" Mrs Gamotte called back.

IT FALLS INTO PLACE

"When are you going to put me into a story, Philip?"

Aunt Caroline came to the dockside to say goodbye, looking like an elderly wax doll topped with a russet and silver wig. She raised her white hands as if she expected me to lift her up and plant her in the middle of some fantastic tale. Faintly mocking though it was, her remark was a kinder recognition of my writer's existence than a postcard I had just received: You are a traitor to your class and to the family, and will be as much disliked back home as Mr Somerset Maugham was in Malaya.

"Yes – when are you going to put me into a story?"

I mumbled something evasive about working on a biography. Aunt Caroline didn't seem like a character anyway: she was too douce and evasive. Perhaps she always seemed flat and shadowy because she lived pressed between the leaves of books: reading was her one great passion. However, she had given me a lightweight Panama hat to emphasise her broad-mindedness, and cautioned me against sunstroke. I was wearing this hat when I arrived on my pilgrimage to the poet Chrysostome's home.

For in the land of my birth a poet had been born, spent the greater part of his life, and died in anguish and frustration. Only a few people in France (his father's country) read his works nowadays – those five volumes of poems so exquisitely produced and bound that they seemed like rare private editions. Two generations of romantic adolescents had never heard of him though he was the only great romantic their territory had ever nourished. At some time or other, in middle life, he had become a Chevalier de la Legion d'Honneur; some of his less lyrical poems were strongly Baudelairean in tone, but his fantasy had been curbed by religion and an inhibiting courtesy. He had a delicate affection for portraits of little girls and had put them into many of his verses – children with large Creole eyes standing amidst waving fronds of palms, enormous bunches of flowers in their frail hands. He had even (legend said) adopted one of these girl children. And yet, now and again certain lines of his poetry blazed with an authentic tropical heat, as if aquamarine glass had struck flames from the sun. These lines had made me feel warm on dismal wintry nights abroad; I had grown to love the man and his works. It was a great sorrow to me that I could remember him so little.

In fact, even my recollections of our mutual homeland were so faint that this pilgrimage was an exploration of the unknown. I remembered Aunt Caroline lying in a hammock reading Diana of the Crossways. It may well have been that the large damp hand descending from a heavy shoulder and briefly laid on my juvenile head was the poet's hand.

Why was there such a fascination in the thought of an artist dying far from the dearly missed friends of his academic days, dying almost unrecognised and certainly unappreciated, in a hot and barely civilised colony? A curious line kept coming into my head, "Poets who die mad in hot countries…"

I tried to add other words to it, but none came. It was the beginning of a poem, not of a biography; and I could not write poetry. But the image persisted. For it was true that my sought for poet had gone out of his mind.

"He was a great trial," said the gentle lady who had given him sanctuary towards the end, in return for some great kindness of the past. "He became melancholy, and would cry loudly in the night – huge big tears like pools. He felt neglected, and tore up newspapers; he complained of the food, and of being ignored…when he went for walks he would stay away for hours, and I worried terribly."

Her stained-looking face took on a tolerant expression.

"We put up with him because he was a poet, and they suffer more than we do."

"Ah! You felt that, did you?"

"Yes, but I never read any of his writings. No one here did."

I asked her if I could go and visit his old estate; she was one of the beneficiaries under his will and gave me permission. Actually she offered to come with me, if I would hire a car. So one Sunday afternoon we set forth for those fields and groves that he had tangled so felicitously into his verses. But the cultivated strawberries had turned wild and run to stubble. The honeybees had disappeared and their hives were cold, devoured by wood-ants. The orange trees were heavy with fruit that nobody bothered to pick: the land was up for sale. Small blackish pigs nosed around the tiny country house he had built; the encircling river made a whining moaning sound. The adjoining land had been transformed by the government into a leper home.

Everything was overgrown, desolate and wild; nature had taken possession the minute the poet's life was over, and set herself to obliterate his traces. I could not help feeling that there was something inimical to poetry in that estate. When I tried to quote a line or two of Chrysostome's poems to my gentle guide (we stood before the logwood trees, which he had planted especially for his beloved bees), the words would not come. Two hundred acres of tropical vegetation had reverted in less than six years to a jungle; the civilising hand was stayed, and even the birds he loved hid in their shaggy emerald retreats. There was nothing to catch hold of, no clue, nothing. Just a great stirring of ruthless magnificence.

"Why did he die so unhappy?" I asked on the way home. We were driving through a village full of filth and squalor.

"I do not know. He was always missing something."

One cannot write a biography about someone missing something; so I took an interval from my search, and revisited some of the town houses I had known as a little boy. As I strolled around I heard the sharp clack of cricket balls in the public park. A big inter-territorial match was in progress. The sound and the glimpse of white flannels between leafy branches tempted me to abandon the hunt for Chrysostome's spirit and fling myself down on the grass beside the spectators.

◆ ◆ ◆ ◆ ◆

In one of these colonial buildings there lived an English lady: Lady Chanterel. When this tall, elderly aristocrat surprised me by opening her own front door I saw that there were hundreds of books in her house, and was heartened to ask if I could come in, since a relative of mine had lived there in the past.

"But of course," she said. She looked lonely. "I will ring for some orange juice." So it came about that we sat facing each other in the quick-falling dusk, smoking and sipping, and I told her of my mission.

"You have seen Mrs Vaudime?" she asked.

"Yes. I have heard all about the poet's miserable end. And I've been out to the estate. But I can't somehow understand it all."

"I expect I may have something to add," she said. "For he used to come here two or three times a week, right up to the end. As you see, I live very simply. I do not dine at the fashionable hour. But our friend Chrysostome would never take account of that. He started coming here just as you have done tonight – simply announced himself and walked in."

I blushed and squeezed my Panama hat in embarrassment.

"He always went straight to a certain chair and sat there, staring at me. At first I was confused, if not alarmed, and used to postpone my evening meal; for he would never accept my invitation to dine. But after a while I just carried on as if he was not present. I had come to realise that he wasn't looking at me at all."

"Mrs Vaudime said that he was always missing something."

"Precisely. The thing that he was missing was love."

Lady Chanterel got up and led the way to a silvery-dark garden. All at once I knew myself to be on familiar ground. I was a little boy again and I heard the softness of a young woman's voice in brief tropical twilight, a voice speaking lightly to someone further in the shadow.

"He saw me, but did not see me, you understand? He may have seen a white dress and heard an English accent, but he was really looking at someone from his past."

"He was looking at my Aunt Caroline," I said. "Her hammock swung here, between those two trees. She used to read out bits of her novel... Her hair was red, and she was as wilful as Diana of the Crossways – and maybe as virtuous..."

"You are a romantic," said Lady Chanterel, smiling.

"Which is what a poet's biographer should be."

"You are probably right," she said. "It falls into place."

"It falls into place," I repeated. Yes, now I could imagine Aunt Caroline on horseback, a woman at the height of her young maturity, her russet mop waving upwards; I could see her touch the poet's cheek playfully with her riding switch as she spurred her pony and called out between the orange lanes of that teeming jungle: "When are you going to put me into a poem, Chrysostome?" At last I understood the long strain of Chrysostome's nostalgia for France and his friends, and his dramatic attempts to civilise nature.

"She was probably the only full-grown person he ever cared for," Lady Chanterel mused aloud. "Certainly the first." A procession of picturesque young persons with large dark eyes dropped like petals on the grass, merging in one prototype.

Taking my leave like an old-fashioned romantic, I raised the strange lady's hand to my lips to show her that grace and courtesy had not passed with the poet Chrysostome. But I was thinking: I salute you, Aunt Caroline. Aunt Caroline, I salute you. You didn't seem like a character, but because my poet was in love with you to the very end, I am putting you into a story.

Just outside Lady Chanterel's gate I met up with the cricket-pitch crowd. Some of my friends recognised me and started chiding me for moping around, when such a great match was being played.

But what did I care? Long after the cricket score was forgotten, Chrysostome's beautiful melancholic poems would be read, somewhere in the world, and the mystery of his sorrow would be talked of at sunset between friends. I muttered loud enough for the sportsmen to hear: "Never mind whether he was a Frenchman or a Britisher, a coloured man or a white man – he was a great poet, who died unloved, and he will always be one of us."

Postscript

I was very close to Phyllis Allfrey from the 1960s when I began to send her articles and short stories for publication in her Dominica Star newspaper. Later, I joined Phyllis and her husband Robert in the haphazard process of bringing out the little 12-page tabloid every week. Phyllis and Robert were eking out a living by taking in printing jobs and rolling off the paper's stencilled sheets on a rickety and unpredictable Roneo machine that Robert kept together with bits of wire and judiciously placed weights.

The 1970s was a turbulent time for Dominica as it lurched from one political crisis to the next. Phyllis was in her element in the midst of it all as she pounded out political comment and satirical verse on her old typewriter. But in quiet moments she did concede that this was a distraction from her creative work: the poetry, short stories and the second novel In The Cabinet that she wanted to complete. It was also a decade of great personal tragedy for her. I can never forget her howl of anguish as I arrived at the decaying plantation mill that was their home after hearing of the death of their daughter, Phina, in a car accident in Africa. It was a tragedy that deeply scarred her remaining years.

But Phyllis fought on, for a while at least. The Dominica Freedom Party that she helped to found finally became the government in 1980 and Virago Press republished The Orchid House in 1982. This gave some comfort but by the time that The Orchid House was made into a television mini series for Channel 4 in 1990, with all the royalties and kudos that would have been hers, Phyllis was gone. "It seems she simply gave up," said her doctor at the end.

The short stories in this book are from an earlier time, almost all of them written before her return to Dominica in 1953. It was a period that I only knew of from faded photographs, newspaper clippings, mildewed literary magazines and Phyllis's own recollections as she told about some evening with a once famous author, days at British Labour party meetings, or weekends with wealthy, kindly friends in upstate New York. It was a time of creativity and inspiration and conviviality among those who shared her passion. But this was cut short by her return to Dominica and her immersion into small island politics. The bitter acrimony and petty feuds that this engendered seemed to stifle her craft. And yet without it, her four years as a minister in the aborted Federal Government of the West Indies would not have happened, and this was, along with her published works, the high point of her life.

In the midst of this creative paralysis she encouraged other younger Dominican writers who were emerging in a society without a popular literary culture. My own short stories were always given a lift once she had brushed up some awkward phrase or inserted words of her own making, transforming a bland effort into something with extra sparkle which she published and paid two dollars for, from the Star's meagre takings. While she worked on these, her own short stories and poems lay around her as embers from past fireworks of literary achievement, a lingering afterglow that gave her the energy to get through the 1970s and early 1980s.

She would have been thrilled to see this book out, with so many of those stories bound together between two covers for the first time.

"Man, come let us take a drink on that!" she would have said, tossing her head back with a wicked little smile, waving the rum bottle in my direction and glancing misty-eyed towards the blue green hills above.

Profile of Phyllis Shand Allfrey

Looking down from the road above the Roseau River running like a trout stream towards the sea, and across wild fields of citrus fruit, you can make out a tiny, tin-roofed old sugar mill huddled alone under a towering cliff face clad in the startling greenery of Dominica. This is the home of Phyllis Shand Allfrey, born into one of the oldest white families in the Caribbean, poet and novelist, socialist and idealist and one-time minister in the Federation of the West Indies.

Down the muddy drive from the house young men are moving stones and digging ditches. "In our big field the workmen are building a house," says Mrs Allfrey. "It's like The Cherry Orchard. They go clump, clump, clump." Her light voice ripples, its Caribbean tones fused with a very English gentility.

The changing order in Phyllis Allfrey's orchard, once owned by the present prime minister and now by her overseer, finds a poignant metaphor in Mrs Allfrey's own life, which has embraced a yet larger transition: the declining fortunes of colonial families such as hers and alongside that her own singular struggle to fight not against the demise of colonialism but for it.

It is an extraordinary pleasure to spend time with Phyllis Allfrey and her husband, Robert. Phyllis is now 68, and Robert is older, frailer and needs constant care. The living space of their stone-built home, with its corner curtained off for the four-poster bed, is crammed with cardboard boxes, shelves of archive papers, poetry, historical references, forgotten novels on the Caribbean and the latest paperbacks sent from London. Many of these are damaged by damp. "We call it Mildew Valley," says Robert.

Outside, beside a paved yard with its lean-to roof, is a small pond bounded by palms with elephant-ear leaves and blooms of amaryllis. The ground is swathed in ferns and pink and mauve columbine. When the rain comes it hisses as it touches the foliage and the sun still shines.

"Give that girl a drink," says Phyllis and produces a bottle of white wine from the fridge, their only modern aid; the water from the stream must be boiled before it is used. She stops to talk, standing like a wounded bird - tiny, thin arms clutched behind her back. But the face belies the waif-like body; a splendid mound of still blonde hair is piled and drawp 132n back from brave blue eyes.

Phyllis Allfrey's family have lived on Dominica for more than 350 years; in the old days they were a kind of royal family. Her grandfather was Sir Henry Nicholls, a doctor who researched into tropical agriculture and founded the island's Agricultural Society; her father, Francis Shand was the island's crown attorney. One of four sisters, she spent her childhood in Roseau, the island's shore-side capital, a tiny town of French-style verandahs battered by time and poverty. She never went to school for the one girls' school was the Catholic convent; and anyhow her father kept his family apart from other races. "My paternal relations never mixed. My maternal relations were liberal," she says.

The thirties were the days when visitors in great yachts dropped anchor in Roseau to pay respects to the white ruling class and enjoy the cocktail parties and dances of tropical nights. It was with one such family, American millionaires, that Phyllis Allfrey sailed away from Dominica to the cold north.

In her way, she had joined that pattern of journeys and departures endemic to the peoples of the Caribbean. She was 17. "I was adventurous and wanted to see the world," she says. Then she travelled to London where she saw her sister Celia marry a naval officer at Holy Trinity, Brompton. There she met Robert Allfrey, the sailor's brother. They married when she was 19.

They went to the States, to Buffalo, but it was the depression and there was no work. Returning to England in the late 1930s, they settled in Fulham. All those decades later, Phyllis in her island home describes the London years when she became part-time secretary to the writer and aristocratic radical Naomi Mitchison. "I loved her immediately...she was like an Indian squaw." They were glittering, social and, says Phyllis Allfrey emphatically, socialist days. When war came, Phyllis worked as the London County Council's welfare officer for bomb victims. With peace, there was more time to be homesick – she started to write a novel about home.

There had, too, always been the poems, Phyllis's first love. "My poems are the best part of me," she will say. The title of her anthology Palm and Oak anchors the two strands – north and south – of her character. She entered a women's world-wide poetry competition and won second prize with her poem While the Young Sleep. The novel, The Orchid House, was published in 1953 and republished by Virago in 1982. If there were any justice film-makers would clamour for its rights; but then the debilitating nature of Caribbean colonialism presents whites with uncomfortable problems [It was filmed for Channel 4 in four parts in 1991, directed by Horace Ové].

Acutely autobiographical, it tells the story of the return of three white sisters to their tropical island birthplace. It lovingly unravels a tale of great passion in which the dynamics of race, culture, sex and religion are explored through the eyes of Lally, the old black nurse. "Lally, c'est moi," Phyllis Allfrey says, but those who know her life will detect that Joan, the middle sister back from England, burning with political enthusiasm and idealism, is Phyllis. The strong women depicted in The Orchid House are part of Phyllis' own feminism. "Without men they would never be, as it was naked to the eye from the early days. But with or without men they were Madam's daughters, and that means to say that they could be sufficient unto themselves," says Lally in the book. And these days Phyllis Allfrey, now stripped of power, says, "I have made my own society here – I have my own matriarchy."

When Phyllis returned to Dominica in 1954, her reputation in British Labour party politics, her work with the Parliamentary Committee for West Indian Affairs and welfare work with the immigrant community in London had followed her home. "People were saying bad things. That we were communists, wicked communists." (Among her critics was the present Prime Minister of Dominica, Eugenia Charles, although they are now reconciled.) Her work was with the poor and the dispossessed, the agricultural labourers whom she helped organise.

Her political platform grew and she founded the Dominica Labour party. Her style has been described as a typically English mixture of Fabian socialism and paternalism. In 1958, elections were proposed for the newly-formed but still British-ruled Federation of the West Indies, an ambitious political attempt to bring together the whole of the English-speaking Caribbean. Phyllis wanted to stand as a candidate for Dominica. She was in England at the time and had a race to get back by nomination day. Reaching Barbados, she hitched a lift on a Geest banana boat to Dominica. She landed on the quay with a straw hat pulled down over her face, clutching her precious, printed election leaflets. The first thing she heard was the market women saying, "The white woman promise to come back and she don't come." "I lifted my hat from my face and said in patois 'mwen wive' – I have arrived. I felt as if I had already won."

Phyllis Shand Allfrey was now on her way to Trinidad. In Port of Spain, the chosen headquarters of the Federation, Phyllis was made minister of labour and social affairs. A photograph shows Phyllis sitting next to Grantley Adams, the Federation's Barbadian Prime Minister, in a cabinet line-up. "Dem all dead now man," says Phyllis.

The luxuries and formalities of political life would never have meant much to Phyllis Allfrey. Sonia Adeleke, one of her three adopted Dominican children, remembers her childhood in Trinidad. "We had a big car and chauffeur, but somehow Phyllis's car always had to be pushed to get it started. Material things don't bother her. People would go and see her if she lived in a kitchen for other things she has to offer."

The dream of the Federation, with its cultural and racial fusion so dear to Phyllis Allfrey's heart, came to an abrupt and premature end in 1962 when first Jamaica and then Trinidad seceded, and the small, penniless islands had to admit defeat. Phyllis, still angry at its collapse, puts much of the blame on the British government, who lacked the political will and commitment to make it work.

The Allfreys packed for home with no job and no pension. During their absence new politicians had emerged and Mrs Allfrey found her own power undermined. She was soon to be expelled from the party she had conceived. Her opponents found the excuse they needed when, as editor of the Dominica Herald, she ran an editorial critical of party policies. Journalism – though she hated it – remained her political weapon. Later, the Allfreys launched their own little paper, the Dominica Star, a curious mixture of radical politics and creative writing alongside snippets of news with the air of a "court circular". It survived until 1982.

And there was Josephine. The daughter, born, as Phyllis has

written, "of apples and snow" in a New World winter, and named after the Empress Josephine, who was born on the neighbouring island of Martinique and is a maternal ancestor. "Phina" was killed in Africa, where she taught, in a car crash in 1977. The little wooden house on stilts near the Carib Reserve in Dominica, which they were building for her, has never been completed. "We've lost the heart for it now. How can we live with our daughter gone?"

And then two years later, Hurricane David swept in from the Atlantic, found Dominica in its path and in a day left it bare and brown like a petrified moonscape. "All mashed up," as the islanders say. The roof of the Allfreys' home was partially snatched away. They fended for themselves with their cats and dogs and struggled to retrieve the tin roofing scattered over the land and to reclaim their sodden possessions.

There is quiet respect these days for the Allfreys in Dominica. Visitors come and go, bringing shopping and news from the town. The struggle to survive makes time for writing dificult. "Politics ruined me for writing," says Phyllis, who is trying to finish her long-started second novel, In The Cabinet, a continuation of Joan's story in The Orchid House, and, in part, the tale of Phyllis's own political career. She is also delighted that some of her poems are to be published in two anthologies, for Penguin and Virago, next year.

"I'm slow at cooking, slow at writing, quick at talking," says Phyllis as she prepares lunch, which we will eat at a battered old whist table cluttered with jam jars of wild flowers, books, papers. "Give a little wine to this young lady. Yes man, no man." And she calls to Robbie, her stocky Carib son, soon to go to Puerto Rico to teacher-training college, to make the pumpkin soup, which will be served with a great blackened monogrammed silver ladle.

This profile was first published in the Observer magazine in 1984.